Showdown at Bonawa

Jake Bannister, ex-deputy sheriff, and his brother Ward, run the Diamond B cattle ranch in Colorado. When Ward goes missing during a mission to buy quarter horses from the Circle Dot horse ranch in New Mexico Territory, Jake sets out to solve the mystery of his brother's disappearance.

He finds Ward's body buried in the ground between Deano, in the Texas Panhandle and the Circle Dot. He establishes that Ward was killed by men working for a criminal, Craven, who operated from the Box C ranch nearby.

Accompanied by Marian Redford, whose father had also been killed by Craven's men, Jake sets out to bring the gang to justice. It is a formidable task. Can they possibly succeed?

Showdown at Bonawa

Alan Irwin

A Black Horse Western

ROBERT HALE · LONDON

ISBN 978-0-7090-8747-2

Robert Hale Limited
Clerkenwell House
Clerkenwell Green
London EC1R 0HT

www.halebooks.com

Typeset by
Derek Doyle & Associates, Shaw Heath
Printed and bound in Great Britain by
CPI Antony Rowe, Chippenham and Eastbourne

ONE

In the ranch house on the Diamond B Ranch south of Pueblo in Colorado, Jake Bannister and his brother Ward were engaged in conversation. Four months earlier their parents, who owned the ranch, had both died of yellow fever, and Jake had quit his job as a deputy sheriff in Kansas, and had come to help his younger brother run the medium-sized spread.

Ward was just over thirty. Jake was two years older. Both men were around five ten in height, broad and muscular, with fair hair and a strong, square-jawed face inherited from their father. They had a mutual respect for one another and the last few months had shown that they could work in harmony.

They were discussing the fact that the ranch was in urgent need of a new supply of quarter horses for operations on the ranch.

'I was talking a few days ago to Wes Jordan of the Box J,' said Ward, 'and he told me about a rancher called Grant across the New Mexico border who could supply first-class quarter horses. I reckon I should ride down there and do a deal with him.'

Like his brother, Jake was well aware of the importance of maintaining, for efficient cattle-handling operations, an adequate stock of good quarter horses, so called because of their ability, from a standing start, to reach full run in a few strides, and to maintain that speed over a quarter of a mile.

'Right,' he said. 'When are you aiming to leave?'

'Tomorrow morning,' Ward replied. 'Jordan told me that Grant's ranch ain't far from a town called Delano, in the Texas Panhandle. I'll ride there first and find out where the ranch is located. According to Jordan, it's called the Circle Dot. I reckon I'll be back here in five or six days.'

Ward left the ranch early the following morning, camped out overnight, and crossed the border with New Mexico the following day. Then, riding in a south-easterly direction, he crossed the border with the Texas Panhandle, and an hour later he rode into Delano. It was mid-afternoon, and he decided to stay in Delano overnight and ride to the Circle Dot in the morning.

As he rode along the main street, looking for the livery stable, Ward passed a hotel, saloon, bank and stagecoach office. He stopped outside the stable, dismounted and walked inside. Campbell the livery-man walked up from the back of the stable to meet him.

'Howdy,' said Ward. 'I figure to stay in town overnight. Can you tend to my horse?'

'Sure,' said Campbell, a short, wiry man with a cheerful look about him. 'Looks like you've had a long ride.'

'Long enough,' said Ward. 'In the morning I aim to ride to the Circle Dot horse ranch. I was told it ain't far from here.'

'That's right,' said Campbell. 'It's just over the New Mexico border, about twelve miles south-west of here. If you're aiming to buy some quarter horses you couldn't go to a better place.'

'That's what I heard,' said Ward. 'I'm hoping to do business with Grant.'

He took the saddle-bags off the horse, and as he did so a thick wad of banknotes, held together by a rubber band, fell out of one of them to the floor. He picked it up and replaced it in the bag. After telling the liveryman that he would be needing his horse early the following morning, Ward went to the hotel and took a room. After taking supper in the hotel dining room, he went back to his room and turned in early, tired after his long ride from the Diamond B.

During the evening, as was his habit, the liveryman paid a short visit to the saloon for a drink of beer. While there, chatting to his friend the blacksmith, he mentioned the arrival of the stranger with a thick wad of banknotes, who was hoping to buy quarter horses from Grant of the Circle Dot on the following day. The conversation was overheard by the saloon owner Hammond, who was standing behind the bar, close to the two men. While displaying no interest, Hammond listened intently to what Campbell was saying.

The saloon-owner was a well-dressed, prosperous-looking man in his forties, a little overweight. When the liveryman had left Hammond called two men in the saloon, both employed by him, into his private room behind the bar. The two men, Slater and Kennedy, were tough-looking characters, ostensibly hired to keep order in the saloon. Each of them was wearing a six-gun. During the next twenty minutes Hammond gave them instructions concerning an operation he wanted them to carry out the next day.

The following morning Ward went for his horse after breakfast, and rode out of town, following the route given to him by the liveryman. Eight miles from town a low ridge ran across his path, and he headed for a narrow gap in this, which had been mentioned by Campbell. Halfway through the gap, he slowed to walking pace to thread his way through a jumble of boulders scattered over the ground.

He had just passed one particularly massive boulder

when Slater and Kennedy, both masked, stepped silently out from behind it and stood looking at Ward's back. Kennedy was holding a lariat. With precision he dropped the loop over Ward's head, pulled it tight to imprison his arms, and dragged him backwards out of the saddle. Slater ran up and pistol-whipped Ward over the back of his head as he slid over the rear end of the horse. As his victim fell down his head slammed against a piece of rock embedded in the ground.

As Kennedy joined him, Slater was tying Ward's hands and fixing a blindfold over the eyes of the unconscious man. Kennedy walked on and took the thick wad of banknotes out of the saddle-bag. Then he returned to Slater, who was kneeling on the ground, bending over Ward.

'This man's dead,' said Slater. 'He ain't breathing.'

Kennedy knelt down, and confirmed that his partner was right.

'Hammond ain't going to like this,' he said. 'We were supposed to make sure this man couldn't identify us, then leave him alive, but tie him up well enough to give us plenty of time to get away.'

'I reckon it was that second knock on the head that did it,' said Slater. 'What do we do now?'

'We've got to bury the body, well away from here,' Kennedy replied. 'You remember that abandoned mine tunnel north of here that we looked into a while back? I saw a couple of old shovels lying in there. We'll ride there with the body and the man's horse, and dig a grave for him somewhere near there.'

Slater went for their horses, which were hidden on the far side of the gap. Then they slung Ward's body across the back of his horse and headed for the tunnel five miles to the north. They picked up the shovels and buried the body, with Ward's saddle and bridle, on a suitable piece of flat ground near-by. When they had finished there was no indication that the ground had been disturbed. They returned the shovels to the tunnel, then led Ward's horse across the border into New Mexico. They rode west a further five miles before releasing it. Then they rode back to Delano.

In the saloon they handed the wad of banknotes to Hammond, then told him of the death of the man they had robbed. Hammond cursed at the news.

'The last thing I wanted,' he said, 'was for some-body to come nosing around here looking for a missing man. You sure that grave won't be found?'

'We're sure,' said Kennedy. 'We took good care of that.'

'All right,' said Hammond. 'It looks like anybody turning up here to look for Bannister is going to be disappointed. And there's no reason why anybody would suspect us of having anything to do with his disappearance.'

*

On the Diamond B in Colorado, two weeks after Ward's departure, Jake was talking to the foreman Ed Hartley, a trusted friend of the family, who had been ramrodding the outfit for many years.

'I'm worried about Ward,' said Jake. 'He reckoned to be back here a week ago. He'd have found some way of letting us know he was going to be delayed this long. I'll leave for Delano in the morning. Can't say when I'll be back. Will you take charge here while I'm away?'

'Sure,' said Ed, a stocky dependable man in his late forties, who knew pretty well all there was to know about raising cattle.

Jake rode off the following morning, telling Ed that he would get word to him about the progress of his search for his brother. When he arrived at Delano a little after noon he rode up to the livery stable and asked Campbell whether his brother Ward, who bore a strong resemblance to himself, had called in there about two weeks ago.

'He sure did,' the liveryman replied. 'He stayed here overnight and rode off to the Circle Dot the next morning to see about buying some quarter horses. Never seen him since. I figured he'd gone straight back to Colorado from the Circle Dot.'

'Not so,' said Jake. 'It looks like he's gone missing. I'll ride on to the Circle Dot and see whether

11

he turned up there.'

As Jake left the stable, leading his horse towards the general store, Kennedy, on the boardwalk, passed close by him and noted the strong resemblance to the stranger he and Slater had recently robbed and killed. He watched Jake go into the store, leave it a few minutes later, then ride out of town. During a brief, apparently casual conversation he then had with the liveryman, Kennedy learnt that the stranger he had just seen was looking for his missing brother. Immediately, he took the news to Hammond.

When Jake rode up to the Circle Dot the owner came out of the ranch house as he approached. Jake introduced himself to Grant, and enquired whether his brother had called there two weeks earlier to discuss the purchase of some quarter horses.

'No,' said Grant, a big bearded man in his forties.

'Two weeks ago,' said Jake, 'he left Delano after getting information from the liveryman about the location of your ranch. He'd ridden down from Colorado especially to see you. So it looks like he vanished somewhere between here and Delano.'

'I'm sorry to hear that,' said Grant. 'I'll get three of my hands to help you right now to scour the area on both sides of the trail between here and Delano for any trace of your brother. There's still a few hours of daylight left.'

Jake thanked the rancher and rode off a few minutes later with three hands. They reached Delano as darkness was falling, after a fruitless search. Before they headed back to the ranch Jake thanked the hands and asked them to tell Grant that he would be staying on in Delano for a while. Then he took a room at the hotel and left his horse at the livery stable. He told Campbell that his brother had gone missing between Delano and the Circle Dot, and that he himself would be staying on in Delano for a while.

'I'm sorry about the fix you're in,' said the livery-man. 'Is there anything I can do to help?'

Jake was sure that the sympathy and the offer of help were genuine.

'I'm obliged,' he said. 'I'll let you know later. For a start I'm going to begin searching a bigger area tomorrow for any sign of my brother and his horse.'

He left the stable and went to the telegraph office. There he sent a telegraph message to Ed Hartley on the Diamond B, saying that Ward had gone missing between Delano and the Circle Dot, and that he was investigating. Then he went to the hotel.

Over the next two days he combed a wide area, but the search proved no more successful than the previous one. But when he got back to Delano on the second day the liveryman handed him a letter in a sealed envelope, which one of Grant's ranch hands had left with him. The letter told Jake that a

13

stray horse had been found to the west of the Circle Dot. It went on to say that the horse matched the description of Ward's horse which Jake had given to Grant, and maybe Jake would ride to the ranch to take a look at it.

'Something I've got to tend to,' said Jake to the liveryman. 'I'll bring my horse back later.'

It was well after dark whn Jake reached the Circle Dot. Grant took him to a large stable near the house and showed him the horse, which one of his hands had brought in. It was a handsome chestnut with a white blaze down its face. Jake recognized it immediately as Ward's mount. He confirmed to Grant that it was his brother's horse.

'It was found grazing quite a ways west of here,' said Grant, 'with no saddle or bridle and no sign of your brother. But there's no way of telling where they parted company.'

'There's no reason why Ward would have taken the saddle and bridle off between Delano and here,' said Jake. 'Somebody else must have done that. I'm beginning to suspect foul play. Maybe Ward was ambushed on his way to see you. I think I'll go back to Delano and make some more enquiries there. Would you hold the chestnut for the time being, and you and your men keep quiet about it being found?'

'Sure,' said Grant. 'Is there anything else I can do?'

'I'm obliged,' said Jake. 'Not just now, but maybe later.'

Jake rode back to Delano, arriving there just before midnight. In his hotel room, before going to sleep, he decided that his first action the following day would be to see the liveryman and seek his help.

TWO

The following morning, after breakfast, Jake went to see Campbell at the livery stable. He told him, in confidence, about the finding of his brother's horse. He also told him of his suspicion that Ward had been ambushed, robbed and maybe killed between the Circle Dot and Delano.

'You told me,' he said, 'that you saw my brother ride out of town towards the Circle Dot. Did you see anything else unusual around that time, such as other riders leaving town?'

'Not that I recollect,' said the liveryman, 'though Slater and Kennedy did pick up their horses here and ride out an hour earlier. Which way they were headed, I didn't see.'

'Those two, Kennedy and Slater, what do they do?' asked Jake.

'They work for Hammond, the owner of the

16

saloon,' Campbell replied. 'They ride out of town together now and then. Sometimes they're away for a few days. I don't know where they go. They're not popular in town. Keep to themselves, and each of them carries a six-gun. I often see them in the saloon. I usually go in there once a day.'

'I'm getting an idea,' said Jake, 'of how I might find the people responsible for my brother's disappearance, if you're willing to help me. You wouldn't be running into any danger yourself.'

'Tell me what you'd like me to do,' said Campbell, and they spent some time discussing Jake's plan, agreeing the part which the liveryman was to play in it.

Jake returned to his hotel room. Around noon, as he occasionally did, Campbell went to the saloon and ordered a beer at the bar. The barkeep was busy with other customers, and Hammond went behind the bar to serve Campbell.

'I saw that man Bannister going into the stable earlier,' he said. 'Has he found that brother of his yet?'

'No,' the liveryman replied, 'and I can tell you he's mighty worried. His brother vanished somewhere between here and the Circle Dot. And Bannister was telling me that not only has he lost his brother, but a lot of money as well. His brother was carrying in his saddle-bag banknotes to pay for

17

quarter horses from the Circle Dot. But that wasn't all. He had a lot more money in banknotes, stashed away in a hidden pocket on the underside of his saddle.'

'I can see why Bannister's worried,' said Hammond. 'What was the extra money for?'

'It seems,' replied Campbell, 'that the missing man was aiming to ride on to a cattle ranch near Amarillo to buy some brood stock.'

'What does Bannister figure to do now?' asked Hammond.

'He's scoured the whole area without finding any sign of his brother,' said the liveryman, 'and I got the feeling that he's decided to give up the search. He has a ranch to run in Colorado. He told me he's going to rest up in the hotel today and probably ride north in the morning.'

Hammond left Campbell who, a little later, as he was finishing his drink, saw the saloon owner take Kennedy and Slater into his private room. The liveryman went back to the stable, and half an hour later, Slater and Kennedy came in for their horses. Campbell noticed them both glancing at Jake's big bay, in a stall near the front of the stable. As they rode off, he saw that they were heading roughly west.

He walked across the street, stood on the board-walk in view of Jake, sitting at his hotel window, and mopped his brow with a piece of cloth. Then he

18

returned to the stable and quickly saddled one of his own horses. On seeing the prearranged signal, Jake left the hotel by the rear door and came into the stable from the back.

'I held out the bait to Hammond, and I reckon he's swallowed it,' said Campbell. 'Kennedy and Slater just rode off, heading west. I've got this horse ready for you.'

Jake thanked the liveryman, then led the horse out of the rear of the stable. Keeping off the main street he did his best to leave town unobserved. It was not long before he caught sight of Slater and Kennedy, well ahead of him. Using his field glasses, he trailed them at a distance, doing his best to keep them unaware of his pursuit.

He was watching them through his glasses from the top of a small rocky outcrop when he saw them stop outside what looked like a hole in the side of a hill. One of the men walked into it and reappeared shortly after, carrying something. Then they rode back a short distance towards Jake and stopped again. They dismounted and started digging a hole in the ground.

After a while, they lifted something out of the hole and spent some time on what looked like an examination of it. Then they dropped the object back in the hole which they filled up. While they were doing this, Jake moved to another outcrop to the north from which he could still observe them.

He saw them return the items taken from inside the hill, then watched them as they rode back towards Delano. He waited for a while after they had disappeared from view, then rode up to the hillside, found a shovel inside the tunnel and rode to the place where the two men had been digging.

It was not long before his worst fears were realized. He found Ward's body and the saddle. Shaken, he sat by the grave for a short while, then refilled the hole and returned the shovel to the tunnel. As he rode back towards Delano he was gripped by a grim determination to bring to justice the men responsible for his brother's death.

When Slater and Kennedy reached Delano they left their horses at the stable. They saw that Jake's mount was still there. They went straight to Hammond and gave him the bad news that, though they had ripped the saddle almost to pieces, no banknotes had been found.

'Now why in blazes,' said the saloon-owner, 'would Bannister tell a lie to the liveryman? There don't seem no sense in it. You say Bannister's been in town all day?'

'That's right,' said Kennedy. 'His horse was in the stable when we left, and it was still there when we got back.'

'All right,' said Hammond. 'You two keep an eye

on him, and when he leaves town make sure he's heading for Colorado.'

Jake waited until darkness had fallen before riding unobserved into Delano and up to the rear of the stable. He found Campbell inside, and told him of his grim discovery. The liveryman was shocked.

'I never took to Hammond and the other two,' he said, 'but it's a big surprise to me that they're involved in robbery and murder. What are you aiming to do now?'

'Since there's no lawman nearby,' said Jake, 'I think I'll send a telegraph message to the US marshal in Amarillo. He's a friend of mine. I was a lawman for a time and we worked together for a spell in Kansas. Now that we have the proof, I'll ask him to arrange for the law to come here and arrest Hammond and the others. I'll stay here in town till they turn up.'

Jake went to his hotel room to prepare the message to be sent off when the telegraph office opened the following morning. When finished, it read: HAVE PROOF OF THREE MEN ROBBING AND KILLING MY BROTHER NEAR DELANO IN TEXAS PANHANDLE. PLEASE SEND LAWMEN TO ARREST SAME. WILL AWAIT THEIR ARRIVAL AT DELANO. JAKE BANNISTER, EX-SHERIFF STATE OF KANSAS. The message was addressed to: US MARSHAL ABE DIXON, AMARILLO.

In the morning Jake took the message to the tele-graph office. Mason, the operator, was busy trans-mitting some messages, and Jake handed his own over, asking that it be sent as soon as possible. Then, after calling at the livery stable to tell Campbell that the message had been sent, he returned to the hotel, expecting that he might have to wait several days before the law arrived.

When Mason had read Jake's message just prior to sending it, he reread it several times, then rose quickly from his chair, turned a notice in the window to indicate that the office was closed, and went into the saloon by a rear entrance. He joined Hammond in his private room, and showed him Jake's message. As Hammond read it, he cursed and his face hardened.

'I haven't sent this yet,' said Mason. 'Figured you'd want to see it. We don't want the law nosing around here, do we? I've already guessed that the three men mentioned in the message are Kennedy and Slater and yourself. Craven ain't going to be pleased about this.'

'Two things are clear,' said Hammond. 'First, on no account must you send that message. Second, we've got to get rid of Bannister. We know he's aiming to stay in town till the law gets here. I'll send Kennedy to tell Craven at the ranch exactly what's happened here, and to ask him what he wants us to do about Bannister. He can take that message for

Craven to see.

'And come to think of it, maybe the liveryman's been helping Bannister. Maybe he knows what's in that message. We'll ask Craven about him as well.'

'All right,' said Mason. 'Let me know what he says.'

When Mason had left, Hammond called Kennedy in and showed him the telegraph message. He told him to take it immediately to Craven on the Box C, then to tell Craven all that had happened since Ward Bannister had been killed, and ask him what should be done to Jake Bannister and possibly the liveryman, who was suspected of helping him.

The Box C was a small cattle ranch fifteen miles to the south-east of Delano. Ike Craven owned it, but it was run by a friend of his called Jesse Harvey. Craven was an outlaw who used the ranch as a hide-out for himself and those of his men who were known to the law. Also associated with him were Hammond and his two men in Delano, together with Mason and the stagecoach agent Mulligan.

Craven had helped Hammond buy the saloon, and he shared the income from a crooked gambling operation and from occasional robberies from strangers passing through the town. Mason was paid for any information contained in telegraph messages which would be of use to Craven in connection with his criminal activities. The stage-coach agent Mulligan was paid for advance information on valuable shipments by stagecoach, which then became possible targets for robbery by the Craven gang.

Craven was a bearded man in his forties, of average height and powerfully built, with a bleak, cruel face. He read the telegraph message handed to him by Kennedy, then listened with mounting irritation to Kennedy's account of recent events in Delano.

'I don't like it,' he said. 'The rancher should never have been killed. But now it's happened, we've got no choice. Bannister and Campbell have both got to die. Tell Hammond to deal with the liveryman. It's got to look like an accident. I'll deal with Bannister myself. You and Slater capture him without anybody in town knowing, and bring him here.'

When Kennedy arrived back in Delano late in the evening he repeated Craven's instructions to Hammond.

'We'll deal with Bannister first,' said Hammond. 'Somehow, we'll have to lure him out of town before we capture him. I'm beginning to get an idea of how we might do that, with a little help from the telegraph operator. I'll let you know when I've worked out a plan.'

Early the following afternoon Jake was just finishing a meal in the hotel dining room when the telegraph operator came in and handed him a message. He opened it. The sender was shown as: US

MARSHAL DIXON, AMARILLO. It read: RANGER CAPTAIN AMARILLO ADVISES THREE TEXAS RANGERS RIDING SOUTH ALONG NEW MEXICO BORDER. WILL CALL AT BENDERS CREEK FOR SUPPLIES AFTERNOON OF THURSDAY 17. SUGGEST YOU INTERCEPT THEM THERE AND SHOW THIS MESSAGE. RANGER CAPTAIN AUTHORIZES THEM TO HELP YOU IN EFFECT-ING IMMEDIATE ARREST OF THREE MEN AND DELIVERY TO AMARILLO FOR TRIAL.

Relieved to have received such an early response, Jake took the message to the livery stable and showed it to Campbell.

'D'you know where Benders Creek is?' he asked.

'Sure,' the liveryman replied. 'Take the same route that you followed to the Circle Dot, but when you reach the border, follow it south for about three miles. It's a small settlement. Only a few buildings.'

I'll ride there in the morning then,' said Jake, 'and wait for the rangers to turn up some time in the afternoon. Then I'll ride back here with them to arrest Hammond and the others.'

'Kennedy and Slater rode out of town this morn-ing,' said Campbell, "but they told me they'd be back tomorrow afternoon.'

The following morning Jake rode out of Delano on his way to Benders Creek. As he was passing through the gap in the ridge where his brother had been robbed and murdered, he was captured by

25

Kennedy and Slater, using exactly the same tactics they had used before. When Jake came round, with his hands bound, he was ordered to mount his horse and led off in the direction of the Box C.

THREE

After his capture by Kennedy and Slater, Jake could see that they were leading him in an easterly direction, and wondered where they were taking him. He was almost certain now that the telegraph message he had received was a fake, and that the telegraph operator was in cahoots with Hammond. Which meant that his message to US Marshal Dixon had never been sent.

They had been riding for an hour and a half when Jake saw that they were approaching the buildings of a small cattle ranch. They passed under an arch on which the name of the ranch: BOX C was displayed, and rode on towards the house. Craven and Harvey came out as they stopped outside. Craven eyed the prisoner with grim satisfaction.

'So you're Bannister,' he said. 'You signed your own death warrant when you started nosing around

27

after your brother disappeared. I'm going to find a way of getting rid of you so that no friend or family member, or the law, will ever find out if or where, when and how you died.'

He turned to Harvey. 'In the meantime, put the prisoner in the spare bedroom,' he said, 'and have him tied up good, with a hand in the room guarding him day and night. We can't risk him getting free.'

Kennedy and Slater rode back to Delano and told the liveryman that they had been able to return much earlier than expected. Then they went to report the day's events to Hammond.

'Good,' he said. 'Now you can take care of Campbell. Let's talk about how you're going to tackle the job.'

After a plan had been decided Kennedy and his partner had a meal, then went along to the stable a little before the time that the liveryman usually went into his living-quarters behind the stable to make a meal for himself. Apart from them, the street was deserted. They walked inside the stable and told Campbell that they needed their horses.

'I'll bring them out,' he said, wondering where they were going at that time in the evening.

He walked towards the stall containing Kennedy's horse. Kennedy, walking close behind him, took from inside the sleeve of his vest a short length of stout iron bar. Before the liveryman reached the door of the stall, Kennedy, using all his strength, smashed the bar against the side of Campbell's head. The force of the blow crushed the liveryman's skull; he collapsed on the floor and died almost immediately.

Kennedy went into the stall and put a halter on his horse. He led it out into the open area of the stable and tied it to a post. Then he went to the body lying on the floor and ran his fingers through the blood on his victim's head. He returned to his horse and smeared the blood over one of its rear hoofs, close to the shoe. He wiped his hands on a piece of rag which he hid in a corner. Then he walked to Slater at the door, where he had been standing, ready to warn his partner if he saw anyone approaching the stable.

'It's done,' said Kennedy. 'Now you can go and ask Doc Madison to come along here to take a look at Campbell.'

Slater returned with the doctor ten minutes later. He was a pleasant, popular man, short and slim, and in his late fifties. He knelt down by the liveryman, and took one look at the wound on his head. Then he stood up.

'Nothing I can do,' he said. 'He must have died instantly. What in blazes happened here?'

'We can only guess,' said Kennedy. 'Me and Slater came in to tell Campbell that we'd be wanting our horses early in the morning. We found my horse tied to the post there, and Campbell lying on the floor behind it. That's a good horse, but everybody knows it's purty high-strung and spirited. Even tries to buck me off now and again when I climb into the saddle.'

'Yes, I've noticed that,' said the doctor.

'I looked at that wound,' said Kennedy, 'and I reckon a kick from the horse could have caused it. Maybe the liveryman accidentally frightened it, and it lashed out and hit him.'

He walked up to his horse and looked down at the rear hoofs. Then he took an oil lamp which was hanging on the wall and returned to the horse. He held the lamp near the rear right hoof. The blood on it was clearly visible.

'Take a look at this, Doc,' he said.

Madison walked up to him and looked down at the blood on the hoof. 'It looks like you're right,' he said. 'There's no doubt a kick on the head from a horse could be fatal. We're going to miss Campbell. He was a good man. I'll go and tell the undertaker to collect the body. Nothing more I can do here.'

When the doctor had left Kennedy put his horse back in the stall and collected the piece of blood-stained rag and the iron bar which he had hidden near it. Then he and Slater went to tell Hammond of the success of their plan. He told Kennedy to ride to the Box C early the following morning to tell Craven that the liveryman had been eliminated.

On the Box C Jake spent the night tied up in the bedroom, with a guard inside the room, changed every four hours. It was clear to him that the telegraph operator and Hammond and his men were associated with Craven in some sort of criminal enterprise which was being jeopardized by his presence. He wondered how and where he was to die.

Craven came up to the bedroom to see him a little before noon.

'Got some news for you, Bannister,' he said. 'Seems like your friend the liveryman in Delano was kicked on the head by a horse. Died on the spot. Nobody saw it happen, but that's how it looked.' He grinned evilly. 'Figured you'd like to know, him being such a good friend of yours.'

Hiding the wave of intense anger which swept over him, Jake looked impassively at Craven, who continued:

'As for yourself, I've figured out the perfect way of making you disappear without trace. There's a hill not all that far from here, with a big cave inside. In the floor of one of the passages leading off the cave is a hole. One of my men accidentally fell through this while we were taking a look round. We couldn't hear any sounds coming from him, so we tied some ropes together and lowered a man down to look for him. He was lying dead on a rock surface

31

about fifty feet down. So what we'll do is drop you through that hole. Maybe you'll die instantly. But I'm hoping you'll live on for a while after you've hit the bottom.'

Jake was sure that his fate was intended to be exactly as just described by Craven. He decided that he must make every effort to escape before reaching the cave.

'I'm curious,' he said, 'about the kind of criminal operation you're running.'

'No harm in telling you,' said Craven, who had a fondness for hearing his own voice. 'We ain't fussy. On the face of it, the Box C is just an ordinary small cattle ranch. But from it we carry out all kinds of robberies, including bank and stagecoach robberies and rustling.'

'So that's why the telegraph operator's in your pay,' said Jake.

'That's right,' said Craven, 'and the stagecoach agent as well. They're both very well paid for the information they hand out to us.'

Abruptly, Craven ended the conversation and left the room. Half an hour later Jake was taken downstairs, where two members of the gang, Bond and Turner, were waiting for him. Both men were armed. Jake, his hands bound, was ordered on to his horse. Craven and Harvey stood watching as the two men mounted and led the prisoner off towards the south-east. Turner was leading Jake's horse, and

Bond was riding behind it, so that he could keep a close watch on the prisoner. When they had ridden a distance estimated by Jake to be around fifteen miles, he could see a hill rising ahead of them, with a smaller hill immediately to the left of it. As they drew closer he could see a mark on the side of the larger hill which could be the entrance to a cave. That, he thought, was probably their destination.

With Bond riding close behind him, not the slightest opportunity for Jake to escape had arisen. As they progressed, he saw that they were riding along the top of one wall of a deep, steep-sided ravine which passed between the two hills. There was a swift flow of water along the ravine, but no way of judging its depth.

He made an instant decision. With his hands still tied in front of him, he slipped his feet out of the stirrups, leaned sideways, and fell off his horse. As he hit the ground he straightened out and rolled over sideways until he reached the top of the wall of the ravine and disappeared over the edge as a bullet from Bond's six-gun grazed the top of his shoulder.

Bond quickly dismounted and ran to the point where the prisoner had disappeared. He could see Jake sliding down the steep slope and fired two more shots at him before he disappeared from view over the top of a sheer rock face which dropped down ten feet to the surface of the water. Turner joined him and they waited until they could see

Jake, who had risen to the surface and was moving quickly downstream. Then both men fired several shots at him until he disappeared from view round a slight bend in the ravine. Then they both ran to their horses and, leading Jake's mount, they rode back along the top of the side of the ravine, looking down for any sign of Jake. After riding three miles without sighting him, they gave up the search.

'He's dead for sure,' said Bond. 'Probably drowned after being hit by our gunfire. I'm pretty sure I put two or three bullets into him. What do we do now?'

'Go back to the Box C,' said Kennedy. 'We'll take Bannister's horse with us, like Craven told us to, and tell him that we dropped Bannister through the hole just like he wanted.'

When Jake's feet hit the water, he took a deep breath and stayed under for a short while. When he rose to the surface he was aware that the two men above were firing at him as he floated downstream. Then, just after he had passed round the bend and out of their view, he saw a deep recess in the sheer wall of the ravine, stretching below and above the surface of the water.

Using his feet and arms he managed to manoeuvre himself into the recess, and found a narrow ledge on which he could stand with the upper half of his body out of the water. Standing in that position, he was not visible to the two men searching for him, and his hope was that they would come to the conclusion that his lifeless body was fast floating downstream, and that they would soon give up the search.

Apart from the bullet graze on his shoulder, he had been hit twice, and he suspected that bullets were lodged near his left shoulder and in his left side. Balanced precariously on the narrow ledge, facing the wall, he saw, just above his head, a slight projection from the rock wall which might help to free his hands. He raised his arms and started moving them up and down so that the rope holding them together was rubbing against the sharp edge of the projection. Mindful of the danger of losing his balance and falling backwards, and despite the intense pain in his shoulder and side, he continued until the rope finally parted.

It would soon be dark, and he had heard no sounds above since he had taken refuge in the recess. He judged that it would be safe for him now to look for a way out of the ravine. He left the ledge and floated downstream with the current. After about a mile, he came to a point where one side of the ravine sloped gently down to the water, and here he managed to climb out on to the slope.

For a while he rested there, then slowly made his way up to the top. Here he took a look at his wounds. He was sure that a bullet, having entered from the rear, was lodged near his shoulder blade, but there seemed to be only a slight loss of blood from the wound. Another bullet had entered his side, and the blood flowing from this wound had stained his shirt and vest. He formed a pad with his bandanna and held it over the wound.

He knew he needed help if he were to survive, and he decided to walk towards the south in the hope of coming across a homestead or ranch where he would find assistance.

Darkness was falling as he rose to his feet and started to walk. The sky was clear, and he kept the North Star at his back as he continued slowly and painfully on his way. As time went on his pace grew slower and slower, and frequently he stumbled and almost fell to the ground. Then, omitting to check his direction from time to time, he started veering towards the east. Eventually he fell down, struggled to his feet again, moved forward a few paces, then collapsed on the ground and lay still.

FOUR

On the Crazy R cattle ranch in the Texas Panhandle it was an hour after sunup and the day was fine. Marian Redford, daughter of Mark Redford, the owner, was preparing to ride the five miles into Bitter Spring, a small town to the south, for a visit to a close friend, the daughter of the storekeeper.

Marian was an attractive fair-haired girl in her early twenties, with no shortage of admirers in the area. As she was mounting her horse, her father came out of the house. Still mourning the loss of his wife, who had died of cholera two years previously, he was a big man, normally cheerful, whose hard work and determination had turned the Crazy R into a prosperous cattle ranch. There was a strong bond of affection between him an his daughter.

Marian told her father that she expected to be back by mid-afternoon. Then she rode off to the south. She had covered barely three quarters of a

37

mile when an object on the ground, some way off the trail to her left, caught her attention. Curious, she left the trail and rode towards it. As she drew nearer she could see that it was the body of a man, lying face down on the ground. There was no sign of a horse nearby.

Quickly, Marian dismounted and knelt by the body. She saw the bloodstains on the clothing covering Jake's shoulder and side. She pulled him over so that he was lying on his back. She saw that he was a stranger to her. Bending down close, she could tell that he was breathing, but he appeared to be unconscious, and did not respond to her voice.

She mounted and rode back to the ranch house at full speed. Surprised, her father, who was talking to a hand outside the house, watched her as she rode up to him and came to a halt.

'There's a stranger lying out there on the range,' she said. 'He's unconscious. He's been shot twice, I think. I reckon he's hurt pretty bad. We need to get him to the house.'

The rancher told the hand to hitch a horse to the buckboard. When this had been done, he and the hand climbed aboard, and they followed Marian to the place where Jake was lying. Redford took a look at him.

'This man's been hit bad,' he said. 'He needs a doctor. Let's get him to the ranch house, and I'll send a man to town to ask Doc Cassidy to get here as quick as he can.'

He and the hand lifted Jake on to the buckboard. When they reached the house the wounded man was carried inside to a bedroom and placed on a bed, where Marian and her father removed his vest and shirt and did their best to clean the wounds and staunch the flow of blood. Then they looked in his pockets for something to identify him. But they were empty.

'A good-looking man,' commented the rancher.

'Yes,' agreed Marian. 'I wonder who he is, and how it was he ended up on our range, without a horse.'

'We probably won't know that till he comes round and tells us,' said her father. 'I reckon he lost a lot of blood out there. There's nothing more we can do till Doc Cassidy gets here.'

When the doctor arrived Jake was still unconscious. Cassidy took a close look at his wounds. He was a short, normally jovial man, in his fifties, well-respected in the area.

'Two bullets to come out,' he said, 'but luckily they're not that deep. And he's lost a lot of blood. I'll dig those bullets out and get some bandages on.'

When this had been done, Cassidy told Marian and her father that he thought no serious damage had been caused by the bullets.

'Now we'll just have to watch out for infection,' he said, 'and wait and see if he comes round. He looks like a strong, healthy type to me. I reckon he'll make it, though he's bound to be laid up for a spell. I'll call in tomorrow to see him.'

During the night Marian sat dozing in an armchair close to Jake's bed, in case he came to during the night. But it was daylight, and Marian was just thinking of leaving to take breakfast, when Jake's eyes opened, and he looked at the unfamiliar surroundings. Then he saw Marian. He cleared his throat to attract her attention.

Relieved, she rose quickly to her feet, walked up to the bed, and smiled down at him.

'Sure glad you've woken up at last,' she said. 'You've been unconscious for quite a spell. How're you feeling?'

'Pretty weak,' replied Jake, 'and mighty thirsty. And maybe I can take in a little food if you can manage that.'

'I'll rustle up some food and drink for you,' said Marian. 'You're on the Crazy R cattle ranch. I'm Marian Redford. My father Mark Redford owns the spread. I found you unconscious out on our range yesterday morning. I'll get the food and drink, then you can tell me and father what happened to you.'

After Jake had satisfied his thirst and taken a little food, he spoke to Marian and her father. He remembered all that had happened up to the later stage of his walk during the night. He gave his audience a full account of events since his brother had left the Diamond B in Colorado.

'That's quite a story,' said Cassidy, when Jake had finished. 'The Box C ain't all that far from here. I've heard of Harvey, who's supposed to own the spread, but I've never met him.'

'I found out when they were holding me there,' said Jake, 'that the outlaw Craven owns the place, but Harvey runs it for him. And here's something might interest you. Craven told me that as well as robbing banks and stagecoaches the gang did some cattle-rustling as well.'

'That *is* interesting,' said the rancher. 'I've lost cattle now and again, and so have other ranchers around here. And we've never been able to catch the rustlers or get the cattle back. Maybe this Craven gang is responsible.'

'That's very likely,' said Jake.

'You're welcome to stay here till you're fit to leave,' said Redford. 'What are you aiming to do when that time arrives? I can loan you a horse and some money to help you get started.'

'I'm mighty obliged to you,' said Jake. 'I figure to ride to Amarillo and see Dixon, the US marshal. He's a friend of mine. When I've told him all I know, he'll make arrangements for the law to move in to close down Craven's operation and take him and his men into custody. While I'm in Amarillo I'll pay a visit to the manager of a bank, and have funds transferred there from Colorado.

'But there's one thing worrying me. Just now, I'm sure that Craven thinks I'm dead. But if he got to know that I'm here, that would put you in serious danger. He just can't afford to have me getting in touch with the law.'

'I can see the danger,' said Redford, 'but I have a few men on my payroll who'd be willing to help me guard you till you're fit to leave.'

'I don't want to risk anybody here getting hurt,' said Jake, 'so I've made up a story which can be passed around. The story is that I'm a cattleman called Jackson, from Colorado. I was on my way to Amarillo when I was ambushed by a couple of masked men. When I tried to resist, they shot me twice. Then they robbed me and took my horse. I managed to walk on to the Crazy R, then passed out. How does that sound to you?'

'There's no reason why it shouldn't be believed,' said Redford. 'That's the story we'll pass around, then. Up to now, only me and Marian know the truth. We'd better keep it that way.'

'I think Doc Cassidy should know it as well,' said Marian. 'He's a good friend. I don't think we should lie to him.'

'Marian's right,' said Redford. 'Cassidy can be trusted absolutely.'

'All right,' said Jake. 'We'll tell him when he gets here.

When the doctor arrived in the afternoon, he

examined Jake's wounds and rebandaged them.

'All's well so far,' he said. 'If you carry on like this, you should be able to leave in two or three weeks, though your shoulder could be stiff for a while after that.'

Jake told Cassidy the true story of the events which had brought him to the Crazy R. Then he gave him the story which was to be passed around.

'OK,' said Cassidy. 'If anybody asks me, that last story is the one I'll tell them.'

Jake improved steadily over the following days. Marian spent a lot of time talking with him, and a mutual attraction developed. Sixteen days after his arrival on the Crazy R, though not yet sufficiently recovered to ride a horse, Jake accompanied Marian into Bitter Spring on the buckboard, and went into the general store with her.

He bought a few small items, then left Marian there while he went to the telegraph office to send a message to Ed Hartley on the Diamond B. The message informed Ed that he had found Ward's body, that he knew who killed him, and that he was going on to Amarillo to contact the law and ask them to deal with the persons responsible. After leaving the telegraph office Jake went back to join Marian at the store. He met her friend, the storekeeper's daughter, and the three of them spent some time in conversation in the living-quarters behind the store, before Jake and Marian returned to the ranch.

When Jake had walked from the store to the telegraph office in Bitter Spring he had crossed the
street in front of the hotel. In the hotel dining
room, seated at a table by a window overlooking the
street, was Kennedy, one of the men who had killed
Jake's brother. He had ridden in from the north, on
his way to Amarillo. He had been sent by Craven to
collect some information in connection with a bank
robbery being planned by the outlaw. He was
intending to stay overnight in Bitter Spring.

He glanced out of the window and stiffened as he
stared disbelievingly at Jake, only a few yards away.
There was no mistaking the fact that he was looking
at a man who was supposed to be dead. He watched
as Jake went into the telegraph office and, a little
later, came out and went into the store next door.

Quickly, Kennedy went up to his room and kept
watch on the store. An hour later he saw Jake come
out with a woman. They both climbed on to a buckboard and drove off to the north.

Shocked by his sighting of Jake, and realizing the
serious implications of his escape, Kennedy sat
down to consider what action he should take. Half
an hour later he went to the telegraph office on the
pretext of enquiring about the current charges for
sending telegraph messages. He noticed beside the
operator a thin vertical metal spike fixed to the

table. The operator was holding a sheet of paper on which was written the message he had just transmitted. Kennedy saw him push the sheet down over the spike to join others that had been impaled in the same way. Among these, he guessed, would be a sheet carrying the message handed in by Bannister. Looking round the office, which was a small building standing on its own, he saw that there was a rear door, flimsy in appearance, which could easily be forced open from the outside. As he left the office he looked at a notice on the front door which indicated that two hours later the office it would be closed until the following morning.

He went to the saloon and spent some time at the bar, drinking. Business was slack and the bartender was a naturally loquacious man. Without appearing to be too inquisitive Kennedy soon heard the full story of the circumstances of the arrival of Jake, alias Jackson, at the Crazy R.

'Jackson was in town today with Marian Redford,' said the bartender. 'I heard he'll be leaving for Amarillo in three or four days.'

Kennedy stayed in the saloon gambling until late in the evening. Then he walked along the deserted street to the telegraph office and went round to the back. He threw his body at the door. It gave way at the second attempt. He waited awhile to make sure that the noise had not attracted attention. Then he went inside, pushing the door to behind him. He pulled the blind down over the single window, lit an oil lamp, turned it down low, and looked through the messages on the spike.

He found just one from Jake, addressed to the foreman of the Diamond B. He memorized its contents, and replaced all the messages in the correct order on the spike. He opened the three drawers in a small chest standing under the table, and disturbed their contents. Then he returned the lamp to its former position, extinguished it, left the office, and went to the hotel.

Early the following morning Kennedy left Bitter Spring, heading for the Box C. He knew that Craven would want to know that Bannister was still alive and intending to ride to Amarillo in a few days time to see the US marshal there. As Kennedy was leaving town the telegraph operator arrived at his office to open it for business. As he went in he saw that the rear door had been forced. After checking the contents of the office, he concluded that the intruder must have been looking for cash, and must therefore have been disappointed, since he never left cash there overnight.

When Kennedy reached the Box C he found Craven in the house. He told him that Bannister was alive and was staying on the Crazy R. He repeated the contents of the telegraph message which Jake had sent to his foreman.

Craven exploded with rage. 'Damn Bond and

Turner!' he said. 'Go find them and bring them here right now.'

When Kennedy returned with the two men, he took them into the room where Craven was waiting. Angrily, the gang leader spoke to them.

'I've just heard that Bannister's still alive,' he said, 'and aiming to cause us trouble. You said you'd dealt with him the way I told you to. What I want from you is the truth. What actually happened?'

Bond decided it was futile to lie any further. He told Craven the truth about what had taken place.

'We were plumb sure he was dead,' he said. 'We both sent bullets into him. And when he fell down into the gorge his hands were tied.'

'You're a couple of incompetent fools,' said Craven. 'If Bannister gets to see the US marshal in Amarillo, we're in real trouble. He's got to be killed before he gets there. I'm going to give you two a second chance. And Kennedy will go with you to help out. Your job will be to kill Bannister before he leaves for Amarillo. And do it as soon as you can. We don't want him sending any more telegraph messages. If there's nobody else around when you kill him, take the body to the cave, and hide it there like I told you to in the first place.'

The three men left the Box C twenty minutes later, on their mission to kill.

FIVE

When Kennedy was in Bitter Spring earlier, he had
found out the exact location of the Crazy R Ranch,
and he knew that, as well as Redford and his daughter, a foreman and four hands were living there.
The three riders headed for the ranch, bypassing
Bitter Spring. It was an hour before midnight when
they arrived in the vicinity of the ranch house, and
saw the lights from some of the buildings. They
waited until these were extinguished, discussing
their plan for the forthcoming operation, of which
Craven had put Bond in charge.

They waited a further hour, then, leaving their
horses picketed not far from the buildings, the
three men walked silently up to the house. Finding
the door unlocked, they went inside and lit an oil
lamp standing on a table. They checked the ground
floor for sleeping accommodation, but found none.
Silently, carrying the lighted lamp, and each hold-

ing a six-gun, they climbed the stairs leading from the living room to the bedrooms. The stairs gave access to a passage leading to three bedrooms, all on the right. Unbeknown to the intruders, Redford was in the first, Jake in the second, and Marian in the third. At the time, all three doors were closed.

Slowly, Bond opened the door of the first bedroom, and went inside, followed by Turner, who placed the lamp on a table near the door. Kennedy stayed in the passage outside. Redford stirred, opened his eyes, and saw the two men in the room. Startled, he swung his legs over the side of the bed and sat up, just as Bond jammed the barrel of his six-gun into the left side of the rancher's neck.

'Make a noise, and you're dead,' he said. 'Tell me where Bannister is, and you'll stay alive.'

The rancher guessed that the men had been sent by Craven to kill Jake, and that the lives of himself and his daughter could also be at risk. On an open shelf, in a small chest by the side of his bed, he kept a loaded Colt .45 revolver which he very seldom carried with him. With his right hand, which was out of sight of Bond and Turner, he felt for the weapon, pulled it out, and cocked it, masking the sound with a cough.

'I'm waiting,' said Bond, jabbing the muzzle further into Redford's neck. 'Where is Bannister?'

The rancher brought the six-gun up, and sent a bullet into Bond's heart. Then he tried to jerk his head away from Bond's gun. But he was just too late, and Bond's bullet hit him in the neck. Both men, who had fired simultaneously, were fatally wounded, and collapsed on the floor. Hurriedly Turner took a look at them. Then he turned and ran back to the door and into the passage, taking the lamp with him.

'Bond's done for,' he said to Kennedy, 'and that ain't Bannister in there. Quick. We'll check these other rooms. Bannister's bound to be in one of the other bedrooms.'

Jake had only been half-asleep when he heard the sound of gunfire in the next room. He jumped out of bed and ran to a chest standing against the wall. From the top drawer he took out a six-gun which he had purchased in Bitter Spring. He knew it was loaded. He moved to the door, jerked it open, and erupted into the passage. He saw Turner, holding the lamp, just a few feet away. And behind the outlaw he caught a glimpse of Kennedy.

He fired instantly at Turner who, shocked by Jake's sudden appearance, fired hurriedly and just missed his target. Turner was hit in the chest. He dropped the lamp and the six-gun, and sagged against the wall. Kennedy lost his nerve and, partly shielded by Turner, he twisted round and ran down the stairs. Jake sent a bullet after him which lodged in his upper back.

Marian, in a deep sleep, had only been partly

awakened by the shots in her father's bedroom. She was fully roused by those in the passage outside her door. She left her room, carrying a lighted lamp, to see a body on the floor, and Jake smothering with a blanket the flames rising from burning oil nearby. He motioned to her to wait until he had finished. Then he went up to her.

'This dead man on the floor was sent by Craven,' he said, 'and another one has escaped. We must see if they have harmed your father.'

They went into Redford's room, where Jake's worst fears were realized when they found the two dead bodies. Severely shocked, Marian sat on a chair, while Jake comforted her. But she was a strong, resilient character, and although deeply distressed by the loss of a loving father, she quickly pulled herself together.

'I'm feeling responsible for this,' said Jake. 'If I hadn't been here this would never have happened to you.'

'You mustn't feel that way,' said Marian. 'The one to blame is that villain Craven.'

Jake took her downstairs to the living room, then went to rouse the foreman Josh Ellison, who had a small cabin near the bunkhouse. Josh had worked for Redford since he set up the ranch, and they were close friends. He and the men in the bunkhouse had not been disturbed by the distant gunfire. He opened the cabin door in response to

Jake's knocking, and listened with deep concern and anger to Jake's brief account of the recent tragic event in the ranch house.

'The man Kennedy who got away,' said Jake. 'I reckon I hit him, but maybe he weren't hurt bad enough to stop him riding off. All the same, I'll take a look, to make sure he ain't still around here.'

'I'll get the hands to do that,' said Ellison, who had hurriedly dressed. I'll make sure they're armed, and warn them to be careful.'

Jake rejoined Marian in the house, and the foreman came in a little later.

'Craven has got to be made to answer for this,' said Jake. 'I think I should set out for Amarillo right now, and get Marshal Dixon to send a posse to the Box C as quick as he can. If they move fast enough, they might be able to pick up Craven and the others.'

'Yes, you should do that,' said Marian. 'You'll come back here and let us know what's happened?'

'Just as soon as I can,' Jake replied. 'I expect I'll be riding with the posse.'

As Jake was preparing to leave, a hand came in to tell them that there was no sign of Kennedy, but two saddled horses had been found picketed about sixty yards from the house, and close inspection of the ground with the help of a lamp indicated that a third horse had been tied there. It also revealed a few spots of blood on the ground.

'So Kennedy's ridden off,' said Jake. 'I'd best be leaving.'

He rode through the night, making the best time possible, and reached Amarillo around noon. He soon found the office of the US marshal, and tied his horse outside. He opened the door and stepped in. Dixon was seated at his desk. He was a tall, well-built man a little older than Jake, with a keen eye and a neat black moustache. He glanced up as Jake came in, and his eyebrows shot up. He rose to his feet and walked round the desk.

'Jake!' he said, shaking hands. 'What in blazes brings *you* here?'

As Jake quickly explained the reasons for his presence there, the marshal listened with mounting interest.

'So I'm hoping,' said Jake, in conclusion, 'that you can get a posse together quickly, to ride to the Box C. And I'd sure like to go along with them.'

'What you've just told me,' said Dixon, 'explains why we've never been able to catch up with the Craven gang, even though we were pretty sure they were involved in a lot of robberies in the Panhandle north of here. Let's go and see Ranger Captain Fuller.'

They went into Fuller's office, a little way along the street, and Dixon introduced Jake to the captain.

'Jake here's got some mighty interesting news,'

he said. 'I'll let him tell you himself. I reckon we'll have to work together on this.'

Jake repeated what he had already told the marshal. Fuller listened with considerable interest. He was a short, middle-aged man with a decisive manner.

'I can see we need swift action here,' he said, when Jake had finished. 'I have four rangers available at this moment. Can you help me out, Abe?'

'I happen to have a couple of deputy marshals who just rode in this morning,' said Dixon, 'and I aim to deputize Jake here.'

'Right,' said Fuller. 'My men will be ready to leave one hour from now. I'm putting Ranger Baxter in charge. He'll have orders to take into custody all men on the Box C, as well as Kennedy and Slater, and Hammond the saloon owner in Delano.'

'Right,' said Dixon. 'My men and Jake will be ready to ride in one hour.'

The posse rode steadily northwards during the rest of that day and the following night, with only a few hours' rest before dawn. Then they continued. At one hour after midday, they came within sight of the Box C buildings.

When Kennedy left the ranch house on the Crazy R, with the bullet wound in his back, his one thought was to get back to the Box C to tell Craven that the attempt on Bannister's life had been unsuccessful, that Bond was dead, and that Turner had been shot and was possibly dead also. He headed north at a pace which was restricted by the severity of the pain in his back, and he was slowly losing blood. When dawn came he realized that unless his wound was tended to he was not going to make it to the Box C. Seeing an isolated homestead off to his right, he headed for it. As he slowly rode up to the house, swaying in the saddle, the door opened, and a man and a woman stepped out. Coming to a stop in front of them, Kennedy fell sideways out of the saddle, and lay unconscious on the ground.

When he came to it was late in the day. He was lying on a bed inside the house. His vest and shirt had been removed, and a bandage was wound tightly around his chest. As he stirred and opened his eyes, Rachel Bender rose from a chair and walked up to the bed.

'Where am I?' asked Kennedy.

'On a homestead,' she replied. 'I am Rachel Bender. My husband is Hans. There is a bullet in your back. We have tended to it the best we can, but thee needs to see a doctor. Hans will bring one here if thee wishes.'

She noticed that Kennedy was looking around the room, as if searching for something.

'Thee looks for the gun,' she said. 'It is outside. We are Quakers. No weapon is allowed in this house. And we give help to anyone who needs it.'

'I must ride on,' said Kennedy. 'I have friends to the north. They will get a doctor for me.'

'Then thee will have some food and drink with me and Hans before thee goes,' said Rachel.

Kennedy rode off half an hour later, feeling a little better after his stay at the homestead. But as he rode on through the night, his progress became slower and slower, and he had to stop frequently to rest. It was not until an hour after dawn that he slowly rode up to the ranch house on the Box C, dismounted, and collapsed on the ground.

His arrival was seen by a couple of ranch hands, who alerted Harvey and Craven, who were at break-fast. Craven told the two men to carry Kennedy to a spare bedroom upstairs. Then he and Harvey stood by the wounded man, who had recovered suffi-ciently to speak. He told them what had happened at the Crazy R in the early hours of the morning of the previous day. Then he told them that he figured he'd been hit pretty bad, and reckoned that he needed to see a doctor.

Craven realized immediately that a posse might even now be on its way to the Box C. Swift action was imperative.

'Sure,' he replied to Kennedy. 'We'll get you to a doctor as quick as we can.'

Just after Craven finished speaking Kennedy relapsed into unconsciousness again. Craven and Harvey left him and went into the living room.

'You know what this means,' said Craven. 'We're finished here. We've all got to leave the ranch as soon as we can. Tell a hand to ride to Delano and let Hammond and Slater know what's happened. He's to tell them to leave Delano immediately, and rendezvous with the rest of us in Drago, in the Indian Territory. And when you've done that, tell everybody on the ranch here to get ready to leave.'

Craven returned to the bedroom, where Kennedy was lying with his eyes still closed. He stood looking down on the wounded man. Taking Kennedy with them, with the object of getting him to a doctor in the Texas Panhandle would, he was aware, seriously slow them down. And Kennedy knew far too much about Craven's criminal operations and connections to be left behind for the law to interrogate.

He walked to a wardrobe and took out a spare pillow, then carried it over to the bed. As he lowered it down over the wounded man's head, Kennedy's eyes suddenly opened and he saw what was happening. As the pillow came down over his face, and cut off his air supply, he tried feebly to push it away. But he was too weak, and Craven held it firmly in position until all resistance had ceased. He replaced the pillow in the wardrobe, then left the bedroom and started collecting the items he intended to take with him on his flight. As he was doing this, Harvey came in, intending to do the same. He told Craven that

57

all the men were getting ready to leave. Then he asked what was to be done with Kennedy.

'There's no need to worry about *him,*' said Craven. 'I looked in on him a few minutes ago. That was a bad wound he had. He's cashed in. We'll just leave him where he is.'

Just over an hour later Craven and Harvey assembled with all the men on the ranch and set off at a fast pace on a two-day ride to the border, where they could cross into the Indian Territory. This territory was a favourite refuge for criminals on the run. The maintenance of law and order was the responsibility of the US marshal stationed at Fort Smith, Arkansas.

When the posse rode up to the Box C buildings, they found that Craven and Harvey and all the ranch hands had fled. Horse tracks indicated that they had ridden off to the east. Searching through the ranch house, Ranger Baxter and Jake came upon Kennedy lying on a bed upstairs. Jake bent over him. All the indications were that he was looking at a dead man.

'This is Kennedy,' he said, 'the man who got away from the Crazy R. Him being here explains why the Box C has been abandoned. And likely Hammond and Slater will have left Delano.'

They were just turning to leave the room when a slight sound came from the bed. They walked up to it. Kennedy's eyes were open, and he recognized Jake. As the two men bent down over him, he tried to speak, without success. He made several further attempts, with the same result. Then he summoned up all his remaining strength.

'Damn Craven,' he said, his voice little more than a whisper. 'He did his best to kill me with a pillow over my face.' His voice trailed off, and his eyes closed.

'D'you know where he's gone, Kennedy?' asked Jake, urgently.

Twice he repeated the question before Kennedy opened his eyes. Then he repeated it again.

'Indian Territory,' said Kennedy faintly. 'He'll be at Randle's place, near Re—'

His voice trailed off again, and his eyes closed as his head slumped sideways against the pillow. Baxter checked his pulse.

'This time he's dead for sure,' he said. 'Pity he didn't manage to finish the name of the place where Craven and the others have gone. It sounded to me like it started with the letter R, followed by the letter E.'

'That's how it sounded to me,' said Jake. 'Not that it helps a lot. But maybe the name Randle will mean something to the US marshal in Fort Smith.'

'Right now,' said Baxter, 'we need to get on Craven's trail. They don't have much of a start by the look of their tracks. Maybe we can catch up with them before they reach the border.'

After burying Kennedy the posse left, following the tracks of Craven and the others. But their efforts to catch up were unsuccessful, and they halted at the point where the tracks crossed the border with the Indian Territory

'This is as far as we go,' said Baxter, then turned to Jake. 'Maybe you figure to carry on?' he asked.

'Later,' Jake replied. 'First, I've got to see how things are at the Crazy R'.

'All right,' said Baxter. 'When we get back to Amarillo I'll send a message to the US marshal at Fort Smith to tell him that Craven and the others have moved into the Indian Territory. And I'll tell him what Kennedy said, and ask him to let us know of anybody in the territory called Randle, who might be harbouring Craven and the others. I'll let you know at the Crazy R what he says.'

Having parted from the posse Jake headed for the Crazy R. During his absence, Marian's father had been buried not far from the ranch house. She was obviously very pleased to see Jake, and took him into the living room. He told her all that had happened since he left the Crazy R.

'If Fort Smith can't identify this man Randle,' said Jake, 'I aim to cross into the Indian Territory and do my best to hunt down Craven.'

'If it comes to that,' said Marian, 'I want to go with you. I've just as much reason as you have to see that Craven pays for what he and his men have done.'

'But Marian,' said Jake, 'you'd lose a lot of home comforts out on the trail, and it could be a very dangerous operation. And what about the Crazy R?'

'You can't talk me out of it,' said Marian. 'As for the ranch, I'm sure the foreman will run it for me while I'm away. And there's one thing I'd like you to do for me before we leave. I can see that I need to be able to handle a six-gun and a rifle tolerably well before we set off. Maybe you could help me with that?'

'All right,' said Jake. 'I can see you're set on this. Let's wait and see what information Marshal Dixon gets from Fort Smith.'

A telegraph message arrived from Amarillo three days later. It said that Fort Smith had told them, firstly, that a watch was being kept for Craven and his men, and secondly, that they had no knowledge of a man called Randle who might be hiding the outlaws.

'So we go,' said Jake to Marian. 'I reckon we should ride first to the place where the outlaws crossed the border, before we go into the Indian Territory.'

After receiving the telegraph message, Jake rode into Bitter Spring and sent a message to his foreman Ed Hartley on the Diamond B. It advised Ed that Jake was going into the Indian Territory in pursuit of Craven and his men.

Over the next two days Jake spent time with Marian, imparting some of his own skills in the handling of a six-gun and a rifle. In Bitter Spring he had purchased for her a short-barrelled Colt .45 revolver, much easier for her to handle than the Classic Peacemaker, with its seven-and-a-half-inch barrel, which he himself preferred. He found her to be an apt pupil.

'We'll leave tomorrow morning,' he said, at the end of the second day, 'and each day you can spend some time practising what you've been doing over the last two days. We'll take plenty of ammunition with us.'

The following morning they left the Crazy R, and headed for the border.

SIX

Jake and Marian crossed the border at the point where the posse had abandoned the chase. Jake was impressed by Marian's determination, and the way she was adapting so readily to the hardships of life on the trail. Time and heavy rainfall had obliterated the tracks left by Craven and the others, and they decided to head due east in the hope of finding somebody who had seen the outlaws.

'It's a slim chance,' said Jake, 'because we don't know which way they headed when they crossed the border. But maybe we'll be lucky.'

Their first chance to make enquiries came on the following day when they rode into the small settlement of Shalako. They stopped at the livery stable. As they did so, the livery man came out and looked curiously at the two riders.

'Howdy,' he said. 'You want to stable those horses?'

'Just riding through,' Jake replied. 'But maybe you can help us. Did a bunch of riders, maybe a dozen, ride through here about six days ago?'

'No,' replied the liveryman. 'I'd have remembered that.'

'Thanks,' said Jake. 'We'll get some supplies from the store, then we'll be on our way.'

Jake and Marian had turned their horses, and were riding along the street towards the general store, when the liveryman called them back.

'I've just remembered,' he said. 'The blacksmith rode up to Kansas to visit some kin just over the border recently, and he came back six or seven days ago. He told me about seeing some riders north of here and wondering who they might be. Why not go and speak with him. You can see his place next door.'

Jake thanked him, and he and Marian went inside the shop to see the blacksmith, who was hammering a piece of red-hot iron into shape. He stopped work as they walked up to him. Jake introduced himself and Marian, and said they were interested in the bunch of riders seen by him about six days ago.

'That's right,' said the blacksmith. 'Eleven or twelve riders I'd say, about ten miles north of here, and riding pretty near due east. They passed just north of a high bluff which you can't miss if you ride north from here. I was taking a rest some way north

64

of the bluff when I saw them, and they didn't see me. Would they be friends of yours?'

'Not hardly,' said Jake. 'Maybe you're lucky they didn't run into you. It's likely you saw the gang of outlaws that we're chasing.'

The blacksmith had noticed that Marian, as well as her companion, was wearing a holstered six-gun, and carrying a rifle in a saddle holster.

'I sure wish you luck,' he said. 'Seems like a mighty dangerous job you two have taken on.'

'We've got good reasons for following them,' said Jake. 'When we catch up with them we're hoping for some help from the law. We're obliged for the information you just gave us.'

Jake and Marian bought some supplies at the store, then headed out of town to the north. They had no difficulty finding the bluff mentioned by the blacksmith. They rode past it, and came upon a faint trail running west to east.

'This must be the trail the outlaws were riding along,' said Jake. 'Let's follow it to the east.'

They did this until nightfall, then camped for the night. The following morning they continued eastward, and shortly after setting off they reached a short stretch of ground on which the hoofprints of a group of horses were just visible.

'These could have been made by the men we're chasing,' said Jake.

Five miles further on, they were riding along the

top of a ridge with a gentle slope on the right. On the left was a sheer drop of about thirteen feet, to a ledge about six feet wide. Below the ledge was another, amost vertical, drop to the plain, twenty-five feet below.

Just ahead of them they noticed two animals. As they drew close they could see that they were a mule and a burro.

'There's a prospector around here somewhere,' said Jake. 'If he's been in this area for a while, maybe he saw the men we're after.'

They dismounted close to the two animals, and looked around. There was no sign of their owner. Marian walked to the top of the sheer drop and peered down over the edge. She straightened up and called out urgently to Jake, who was walking towards her.

'There's a man lying down there,' she said.

They both lay on the ground and looked down over the edge. An elderly man, short, slim and roughly dressed, was lying on the ledge. He was not moving. Jake called out to him several times, without getting any response. Then, as he called once again, the man stirred, turned on to his back, and looked up at the two faces above.

'You hurt?' asked Jake, assuming that this was the owner of the mule and burro.

The man's reply was barely audible. 'Busted leg,' he said. 'Can't use it.'

'Don't move,' said Jake. 'We'll bring you up.'

He turned to Marian. 'I saw a coil of rope on the burro,' he said. 'I'll go and get it. I reckon the two of us can pull him up.'

When he came back with the rope he dropped one end down to the injured man and told him to tie it around his chest, under his armpits. When this had been done Marian brought her horse to within a few yards of the edge and mounted it. Jake tied the rope to the horn of her saddle. Then, with Marian's horse taking up the slack as Jake heaved on the rope, the injured man was gradually hoisted to the top of the sheer drop. As Jake pulled him back a few feet from the edge, he could see that the man was in considerable pain, and in a weak state.

'I'm sure glad you two turned up,' the man said. 'I've been lying down there six days, with a broken leg. The name's Sam Logan, by the way.'

Briefly, Jake introduced himself and Marian. Then he examined the leg, which was broken below the knee.

'This needs a doctor, to fix it right,' he said. 'Where's the nearest town?'

'That's Buffalo Creek, east of here,' said Logan, 'about fifteen miles. I called there not long ago. I noticed a doctor's shingle on the street.'

'We'll take you there,' said Jake, 'but first, you must have some food and drink. Going without for six days, on top of a broken leg, I guess you don't

67

feel too good.'

'You're right,' said Logan, and Jake handed him a canteen of water, while Marian whipped up a meal for him. As he was eating and drinking, he told them how he came to be marooned on the ledge on which they had found him.

'Six days ago,' he said, 'I was riding west along this ridge when I met up with a bunch of riders, about a dozen, I'd say. I was taking a meal at the time. They were a mean-looking bunch. They all climbed down off their horses, and the leader told me they were going to take my provisions, on account of they were running out. I was pretty riled over this, and I've got to admit I have a short temper that sometimes makes me do fool things. I pulled my shotgun from a saddle holster on the mule. But I was caught from behind before I could threaten them with it. The leader told me what a fool I was, and he ordered two of his men to drag me to the top of the sheer wall and drop me down over the edge. And that's just what they did. When I hit the ledge, I broke my leg, and pretty near rolled over the edge. They looked down to see what had happened, and I could hear them laughing. Then they stood talking for a while above me, before moving away from the edge. For a while, I could hear faint sounds from above. Then there was silence. The men had ridden off, leaving me with no means of escaping, unaided, from the ledge.'

Jake asked Logan to describe the leader of the group, and it quickly became evident that he was Craven. Jake briefly explained that he and Marian were chasing the group of outlaws who had left the prospector stranded. Then he rode to a small grove of trees ahead and using some of Logan's tools he cut some timber. He took it back to the others and quickly fashioned a travois on which Logan could be taken to Buffalo Creek in reasonable comfort, with some makeshift splints on his leg.

They arrived there, with the mule and burro, just as darkness was falling, and went straight to the doctor's house. Doc Delaney answered the knock, and led them inside. He was a small, brisk man with a cheerful manner. Quickly, he examined Logan's leg, then told his patient that it was a clean break, and provided he rested up for a spell, with the leg properly splinted, it should heal up fine. And meantime he would be able to use crutches to get around.

'Go ahead, Doc,' said Logan. 'I'll have to find me somewhere to stay in town.'

'There's a room and a bed you can have here,' said the doctor. 'You can get meals at the hotel. But right now, I'd better get that leg fixed.'

Jake and Marian waited while Delaney tended to the injury, then they sat with Logan for a short while in the small bedroom which the doctor had offered him.

'You going to be all right here?' asked Marian.

'Sure,' Logan replied. 'It's time I took a break. It sure was a lucky day for me when you two came along. I guess you'll be taking up the chase again now?'

'That's right,' said Jake, 'but it ain't going to be easy finding them, not with them six or seven days ahead of us. We'd sure like to know where they were heading when they left you.'

'Just a minute,' said Logan, casting his mind back to the time just after he had been dropped onto the ledge. 'When I was lying on that ledge, face down and not moving, and expecting a bullet in the back any minute, I overheard two of the men talking just above me. One of them was telling the other about some place they were going to, and a man they were going to meet there. It sounded like one of them had been there before, and the other hadn't.'

'D'you remember any names?' asked Jake, hoping that this was the breakthrough they badly needed.

'Let me think,' said Logan, closing his eyes and wrinkling his brow for a short time before answering. 'I remember the name, because it's the same as the name of a partner I once had. It was Randle.'

Jake and Marian exchanged glances.

'And the place?' asked Jake.

'It was Red something,' said Logan, and once again struggled to remember exactly what he had

70

heard. Then he punched the air feebly with his fist. 'It was Red Rock,' he said. 'Can't say I've heard of it myself.'

Neither Jake or Marian had heard of the place either, nor had the doctor when they asked him.

'There's one man in town who might know,' said Delaney, 'and that's Arnold. He used to drive freight wagons around the territory. Go and ask him. Come out on the street and I'll show you where he lives.'

They found Arnold in his small house on the edge of town, and introduced themselves. He was a grizzled old-timer, still spry despite his sixty-five years. He invited them inside, and Jake asked him if he knew the location of a place called Red Rock.

'Never been there,' said the teamster, 'but I've been near. I know where it is. It's about a hundred miles east of here. I heard that it got its name from a big outcrop nearby that had a reddish tinge to it. And it's the only place I knows of with that name.'

He went on to give his two visitors a more exact location of the town, after which they thanked him and returned to Logan to give him the good news, and tell him that they would be leaving for Red Rock early the next morning. He wished them well.

SEVEN

During their journey to Red Rock Marian, who had proved to be an apt pupil, continued to practise handling and firing her six-gun and rifle. They knew that they were approaching their destination when they spotted, in the distance, the big reddish-coloured outcrop that gave Red Rock its name. As they entered town they saw an elderly bearded man sitting on a chair on the small porch of a shack on their left. He waved as they approached, and they stopped as they came abreast of him. His name was Carter.

'Howdy folks,' he said, closely observing the two riders. 'Welcome to Red Rock. I don't often see strangers riding into town, especially young, good-looking ladies, so I'm naturally curious about what you're doing here. I know it's bad manners to ask, and it might land me in trouble, but I can't help myself. I'm just naturally inquisitive, I guess.'

Jake smiled at him. 'No offence taken,' he said. 'We're just riding through. Might rest up here a day or two. You've got a hotel here?'

'Sure,' said Carter, 'but it's pretty small. Only four rooms. It's further along the street, on the left.'

'That's the only accommodation in town?' asked Jake.

'That's right,' replied Carter. 'We ain't got much call for it here.'

'Are there any ranches around here?' asked Jake.

'Only one,' Carter replied. 'That's a horse ranch called the Open A. The ranch house is about five miles from here. A man called Randle owns it.'

'Is it a big ranch?' asked Jake.

'No,' Carter replied. 'As far as I know, he has around six ranch hands and a foreman.'

He paused for a moment, and looked closely at Jake before continuing.

'It just struck me,' he said, 'that for somebody just passing through, you seem pretty interested in this area.'

Jake smiled. 'Just naturally inquisitive,' he said. They thanked the old man, and rode further along the street. They stopped outside the hotel, dismounted and stood talking for a short while.

'It looks like we've come to the right place, Marian,' said Jake. 'Craven and the others must be hiding out at the ranch. But we've got to be sure of that before we call the law in. I reckon we should

73

take a couple of rooms here, and decide on our next move. What d'you think?'

'A good idea,' she said. 'I'm looking forward to a good night's sleep in a proper bed.'

They went inside the hotel. Parker, the owner, told them he had two rooms they could use, and they could take meals in a small dining room in the hotel. Marian went up to her room, and Jake took the horses to the livery stable along the street, where he handed them over to Emerson the livery-man.

'Me and the lady I'm riding with,' said Jake, 'we're aiming to rest up here a few days before we ride on. The old-timer sitting on his porch back along the street there told me there was a horse ranch near by. What kind of horses do they breed there? I might be interested enough to take a look at them before we ride on.'

'So you had a talk with Hank Carter,' said the liveryman, a middle-aged, stocky man, with a cheerful look about him. 'Hank's a good friend of mine. There ain't many folks riding in from the west that get by Hank without him finding out who they are, and what they're doing here. Before he retired he was a deputy sheriff in Kansas, and before that he was a ranch hand and a trail hand.

'As for the horse ranch, that's the Open A. I know they supply horses now and then to the US marshal in Fort Smith for the deputy US marshals who keep the law in the Indian Territory. And they breed quarter horses as well.'

'Maybe I'll ride out there before we leave,' said Jake.

'It's five miles north of here,' said the liveryman. 'You can't miss it. The ranch house is right close to a big flat-topped hill, standing on its own.' Jake returned to the hotel, and told Marian what he had learnt.

'This man Randle's got plenty of nerve,' he said, 'if he's hiding criminals and selling horses to the law at the same time. It turns out that the old-timer we spoke to on the way in is called Hank Carter. And he's worked as a deputy sheriff. I think we should tell him what we're doing in Red Rock. I reckon he knows everything that's going on around here. Maybe he can help us.'

'You're right,' said Marian. 'Let's go see him in the morning.'

Next day, after breakfast, Jake and Marian walked along to Carter's shack. He invited them inside, and all three sat down. Jake gave Carter a full account of all the events leading up to their arrival in Red Rock, mentioning that he himself had served for a while as a deputy sheriff in West Kansas.

'It seems to us,' he said, 'that it's more than likely Craven and his men are in hiding on the Open A. How does the idea strike you?'

'Myself, I served as a deputy sheriff in east Texas

for quite a spell,' said Carter. 'As for the idea that Randle is sheltering criminals, the thought never came into my head. If he is doing that, he's making a darn good job of hiding it.'

'When did he set the ranch up?' asked Jake.

'About two and a half years ago,' Carter replied. 'He came from Arkansas himself, and all the building work was done by a big Arkansas contractor. Seems they were there quite a while. Nobody in town has seen the buildings close up. Randle's let it be known that casual visitors ain't welcome, and are likely to be shot down. Reckons he's had trouble with horse-thieves. After what you've just told me, the way he's acting *could* mean he has something to hide.'

'Has anybody ever seen strangers on or near the ranch?' asked Jake.

'Never,' Carter replied. 'We see the hands in town now and again, and the cook comes into town every week for provisions. And I think that a freight wagon comes to the ranch from Kansas pretty regular. But I don't know what it carries.'

'It could mean,' said Marian, 'that any outlaws coming to the ranch have been told to arrive during the dark, and they're all kept hidden while they're there.'

'I think you're right,' said Jake. 'We need to take a close look at the place, and it'll have to be during the night. And quite likely they'll have night guards on duty. We'll have to watch out for them. I reckon we might as well ride out there tonight, to check whether our hunch is right.'

'You better be careful,' said Carter. 'Anything I can do to help?'

'We'd be obliged if you said nothing about why we're here,' said Jake, 'and if we don't get back here in five days you can take it that something's gone wrong. If that happens, could you get word to the US marshal in Fort Smith, or one of his deputies, that we've gone missing while checking out what's happening on the Open A?'

'I'll do that,' said Carter, 'and what you've just told me stays with me if that's the way you want it. But I reckon it'd be better if you let me tell the liveryman what you're doing, before you leave. He's a good friend of mine, and I can guarantee he won't talk.'

'All right,' said Jake. 'And thanks for your help. We'll ride off an hour before midnight, and take a look around the buildings when most of the folks on the ranch will be in their beds.'

Before leaving Red Rock late in the evening, Jake and Marian bought some provisions at the store. Then they headed north. They caught sight of the outline of the high flat-topped hill described by the liveryman in Red Rock, although the ranch buildings close to the hill were not yet visible. They stopped near a small grove of trees. The time was close to midnight.

'We're getting close, Marian,' said Jake. 'I'd best go on alone now, and you can wait in this grove. It's likely they'll have night guards on duty, and I aim to locate them, then slip through them and take a good look round. Then I'll come back here. If I don't get back before dawn, you hightail it back to Red Rock and tell Carter what's happened.'

'I was expecting to go on with you,' said Marian, 'but I suppose there's some sense in us separating. The guards will be less likely to spot one intruder than two. But take care. I was getting used to having you around.'

'It's the same with me,' said Jake. 'Take your horse inside the grove with you. I'll be back well before dawn. I'll call out when I'm getting near.'

Jake rode on to a point at the foot of the hill, which was just outside the visual range of any guards who might have been posted outside the buildings. He picketed his horse, then started slowly circling the group of buildings, drawing closer each time. The occasional sound of voices, and now and then the flare of a match being used to light a cigarette, helped him to conclude that two guards had been posted, both outside the ranch house, at the front.

He moved round, then came up to the rear of the ranch house, which was only about six feet

78

from the base of the hill. He noticed that an extension had been built from the rear of the house to butt up against the side of the hill. It was eight feet wide by eight feet high, with no doors or windows. Curious, he examined it, wondering what its purpose might be. Then he moved cautiously to the large cookshack, which was close to the side of the house, and connected to it by an enclosed walkway. He moved on to look at the outsides of the bunkhouse, large stable and barn, then returned to the rear of the house. He was intrigued by the extension to the hillside, and was considering entering the house by way of the cookshack, thus avoiding the guards, in order to take a look at the extension from the inside.

He was moving slowly round the cookshack, looking for the best place to attempt an entry, when he heard somebody shouting at the front of the house. He flattened himself against the wall. Then he heard the voices of several men. Soon after this he heard more voices, and lamps were lit inside the house, followed by someone running past the cookshack towards the bunkhouse. He decided it was time for him to leave. He went back to his horse, then rode to the place where he had left Marian. He called out as he approached, but there was no response. He dismounted and walked into the grove. But there was no sign of Marian or her horse.

When Jake left Marian she sat down among the trees, praying that he would return safely. A short distance to the south two riders were approaching the grove. They were two outlaws, Kelly and Lawton who, on the run from the law, were heading for refuge at the Open A. As they passed a little way off the west side of the grove, they both heard the faint sound of a horse snorting inside it, but carried on without hesitation for a further ninety yards. Then they left their horses, partially circled the grove, and silently approached it from the east. Marian, unaware of the passing of the two riders, was seated in the centre of the small grove, and her horse was tied to a tree close by. The two outlaws, six-guns in hand, entered the grove behind Marian, and moved cautiously towards the centre. The slight sounds they made were masked by the movements of the restless horse, and with Marian still unaware of their presence, they drew close enough to see the dim shape of someone seated on the ground.

The two men grabbed Marian, and took her six-gun, then ordered her to remain seated on the ground. Lawton struck a match and the two men, looking closely at her, realized that their prisoner was a woman. Lawton looked at her horse, and other belongings, including the field glasses which Jake had left with her. Then he spoke to Marian.

80

'We'd sure like to know,' he said, 'what in blazes you're doing here alone halfway through the night, with a six-gun and a rifle. It don't seem ladylike. You should be home in bed.'

'I know it sounds silly,' said Marian, still shaken by the sudden appearance of the two men, 'but I went out for a long ride and got myself lost. I figured I'd best rest in this grove till daylight. My father owns a big ranch not far from here. I guess he'll have men out searching for me.'

'That's a story I find pretty hard to swallow,' said Lawton. 'I know somebody who's going to be very interested in what you're doing here, armed and carrying field glasses. We'll take you along to see him right now. It ain't far to go.'

Marian's hands were tied and she was ordered on to her horse, which was led to the mounts of her captors. Then all three rode to within hailing distance of the Open A night guards. Lawton shouted out the names of himself and his partner, and after a brief interval he was told to ride in.

'Better call Randle,' said Lawton as they reached the guards. 'We found this woman hiding in that grove of trees just south of here.'

'I'll call him,' said one of the guards. 'Bring her into the house.'

The two outlaws took Marian into the living room, while the guard went upstairs to rouse Randle, who joined them five minutes later. He looked searchingly at Marian, then listened while Lawton told him where she had been found alone, and showed him her six-gun and the field glasses.

'She claimed her father owns a big ranch near here,' he said, 'and she told us she went out riding and got lost.'

'Did you see any sign of anybody else having been with her?' asked Randle.

'No,' replied Lawton, 'no sign at all.'

Randle walked up and took a close look at Marian.

'There's no big ranch around here,' he said, 'and I've never seen this woman before. It's clear she's lying.' He spoke to Marian directly. 'I want to hear the truth,' he said, 'and I don't mind how I force it out of you. You may as well start talking right now.'

Marian remained silent. She could think of no plausible explanation, other than the truth, of her presence in the grove in the middle of the night.

Randle decided that when his guests had arisen later that morning, he would see if any of them recognized the woman. Meanwhile, he would hold her prisoner in a spare bedroom upstairs. He told the guard to bring a ranch hand from the bunkhouse to help him take the woman to the bedroom, tie her up securely, and rope her to the bed. The hand was then to remain in the passage outside the bedroom door, on guard, and the night guard was to return to his duties.

The following morning, Randle's guests, all nineteen of them, walked through the extension between the hillside and the house, and took breakfast at a large table in the big cookshack. Then they were told about the discovery of Marian by Lawton and Kelly. They were taken, one by one, to the bedroom where Marian, blindfolded, was seated on the bed. Each one took a good look at her, then went down to the living room, where Randle established that no one there had seen her before.

'She won't talk,' he said, 'but I think she was spying on us for some reason. The question is, what do we do with her?'

'I can see the fix you're in,' said Craven. 'One solution is to finish her off. But that would be a waste. I think I've got a better idea. You know we're leaving today, near nightfall, heading for south-east Texas. We'll be passing close by Nelson's place, not far north of the Red River. We've gone into hiding there a few times before we moved to the Panhandle. I think you know him?'

'I do,' said Randle. 'He's a friend of mine. I know he runs a bigger place than this. Has a saloon and store.'

'That's right,' said Craven, 'and he was always having trouble getting girls for the saloon. If you like, we'll take her along with us, and hand her over to Nelson.'

'A good idea,' said Randle. 'I know Nelson won't

allow her to get away, once she's there. I'm obliged to you.'

Marian, held captive in the bedroom, received food and drink during the day. An hour before nightfall, Randle came into the room and told her that she was to leave the ranch shortly, accompanied by other riders. He gave her no further information, and her heart sank as she realized that any attempt by Jake to rescue her from the Open A during the night would be fruitless.

Half an hour later, Craven and his men, with Marian on her own horse, fearful of what the future might hold in store for her, left the Open A. Just before their departure, Craven spoke to his men.

'I don't want no trouble from you men over this woman,' he said. 'Nobody bothers her on this ride, and I mean *nobody*.'

From the top of a low ridge Jake had been watching the distant Open A buildings, waiting for midnight, when he intended to ride there in an attempt to rescue Marian. Shortly before nightfall he stiffened as he saw a group of riders leave the buildings and head south-east. Without field glasses he was too far away to be able to identify any of them. Five minutes later a lone rider left the ranch buildings, and headed in Jake's direction through the growing darkness.

Jake watched the rider, and could see that he was

heading for a small gap in the ridge not far from where he was lying. The thought occurred to Jake that if he intercepted this rider, maybe he could force him to give information, such as the place where Marian was being held, which would help him in his rescue attempt. He climbed down the ridge to the place where he had left his horse, then walked to the gap and took up a position behind a large boulder, halfway through the gap, to await the oncoming rider. There was just enough light for him to see the outline of the horse and man as they drew close.

Just after the horse had passed him Jake ran silently out from behind the boulder, then up to the rider. He grabbed the man's arm and pulled him out of the saddle, then held a pistol to his head as he hit the ground. He took the man's six-gun and threw it to one side. Then he squatted down, with his gun pointing at his prisoner's head.

'Let's have a little talk,' he said. 'I saw you leave the Open A. I need some information about the place. You can either tell me what I want to know right now, or we can do it the hard way. I've got plenty of time.'

'I've heard that voice before,' said the man lying on the ground. 'What in hell are you doing down here, Deputy Bannister?'

Jake, in turn, thought he recognized the other man's voice. 'Is that you, Lonnigan?' he asked.

'That's right,' said Lonnigan. 'I'm going to sit up. That was a fool thing you did, pulling me off my horse like that. It's shook me up considerable.'

Jake looked at his prisoner. Lonnigan was a crooked gambler and small-time robber whom he had encountered while serving as a lawman in Kansas.

He had once been arrested by Jake for the murder of another gambler, and the evidence against him was so overwhelming that he was sentenced to death by hanging. But after the arrest Jake had become convinced that Lonnigan was innocent. Before the sentence was carried out he had unearthed the proof that the gambler had been framed.

'Like I told you, Lonnigan,' he said, 'I want some information about the Open A. I know you've been there. I know it's a hideout for outlaws, and Randle is holding a woman friend of mine there against her will. I aim to go in and rescue her.'

'That wouldn't have been easy,' said Lonnigan, 'but I'd have been willing to help you, on account of you saving me from the hangman, and on account of the way they were aiming to treat the woman. But she ain't there no more. She left with the Craven gang not long before I rode out.'

He went on to tell Jake of the plan to hand Marian over to Nelson for work as a saloon girl in the place which Nelson had set up as a haven for criminals.

'Where is Nelson's place?' asked Jake.

'I know about it, but I ain't ever been there,' said Lonnigan. 'According to what I've heard, it's in the south-east of the Indian Territory, not far north of the Red River. I talked once with a man who'd stayed there. He told me that Nelson put out the story that he was entertaining rich visitors from the East who wanted a brief taste of life out West.'

'I'm going to follow Craven and his men,' said Jake. 'They ain't got that much of a start, and I saw exactly which way they were heading. I'm going to get on their trail right now. I'm obliged to you for the information.'

'While I was at the Open A,' said Lonnigan, 'I got to thinking again about what a close call I'd had in Kansas, and I looked around at the criminals who were staying there, and thought about the innocent people they'd killed. I got to thinking maybe I could go straight from now on. *You* know I've never killed or hurt anybody, nor stolen from anybody who couldn't afford to lose the money. I'd like to help you. I'd like to go along with you after Craven. You know how the odds are stacked against you, on your own. And this could be a chance for me to make a fresh start.'

Surprised, Jake considered Lonnigan's suggestion. He knew that what he had just said about his criminal activities was true. And he needed all the help he could get.

'All right,' he said, 'but if you change your mind, you're free to part company with me. Now we'd best be moving.'

'I won't change my mind,' said Lonnigan.

EIGHT

Jake, now accompanied by Brad Lonnigan, rode to the point where Jake had seen Craven and the others disappear from view. Then they rode along the faint trail which the outlaws had been following. Jake's hope was that they would camp for the rest of the night, after a few hours' ride.

As they rode along, Brad told Jake about the set-up at the Open A. He said that the horse ranch was merely a front concealing a much more lucrative business of providing accommodation and shelter from the law for twenty or more criminals.

'Where does he keep them all?' asked Jake.

'I reckon you saw how close the buildings are to the hill,' Brad replied. 'And there's an extension from the house to the hillside. There's a door at the end of the extension, very well hidden, that covers the entrance to a cave inside the hill. Randle had had a contractor in there who had enlarged the cave, and built pretty high-class accommodation for his guests. At the first sign of strangers heading for the buildings, all the guests go into the cave.'

'The woman Marian Redford, who was being held prisoner, did you see her?' asked Jake.

'I sure did,' Brad replied. 'Everybody there took a look at her to see if anybody recognized her. But nobody did. She was in a bedroom, blindfolded.'

'Did she look all right?' asked Jake, who had already told Brad how he and Marian came to be on Craven's trail.

'She looked OK,' said Brad. 'No sign of her being harmed, if that's what you mean.'

The two men rode on, hoping that the outlaws had stayed on the trail. A little over three hours later, they saw a glimmer of light ahead, slightly to the left. They stopped when they were about a quarter of a mile from the light. It looked like a campfire.

I'll go ahead on foot,' said Jake, 'and see if the men we're after are camping there. You stay here with the horses. I'll get back as soon as I can.'

Cautiously, Jake advanced through the darkness. The night sky was clear. Soon he could see that the campfire was just a little way off the trail, on a flat stretch of ground dotted with small patches of brush around four feet tall. Bent double, he circled the camp, moving closer in as he did so, and taking advantage of the cover afforded by the patches of brush.

It was not long before he was able to establish that there were eleven people lying on bedrolls on the ground, and two men, presumably guards, sitting on the ground on opposite sides of the fire, a little way back from it. He looked at the figures lying on the ground, but it was impossible to say, in the poor light, whether Marian was among them. He had noticed, earlier, a picket line, well away from the fire, to which thirteen horses were tied. He moved round and approached the line, keeping the horses between him and the two guards. Talking quietly to the horses, which were tied facing away from the campfire, he saw one with a white blaze down its face, which could be Marian's. He patted its shoulder, then felt its right foreleg, just above the knee. Immediately, he felt the small scar which he had noticed many times before. He withdrew, and returned to Brad.

'Marian's horse is there,' he said, 'which makes it almost certain that she's there herself, with Craven and his men. With a dozen men escorting her during the day, we don't stand a chance of rescuing her. And the same applies at night. There are just too many of them. All we can do for now is follow them.'

'You're right,' said Brad. 'It'd be crazy to try anything else. How long will it take to get to Nelson's place, d'you reckon?'

'It's probably a three-day ride,' said Jake. 'We'll

follow as close as we can without them seeing us.'

Next day Brad and Jake followed the thirteen riders, without being able to get close enough to confirm that Marian was in the party. Not long after noon, they saw a small town off to the right. Two men left the group ahead, and rode towards it. The remainder carried on, at a slower pace, in the same direction as before.

'Probably going in for some provisions,' said Jake. 'When they've left, I'll ride in myself. I want to send a telegraph message to Carter at Red Rock. I want to let him know that Craven's left the Open A, and I'm following him. I'll tell him that I'll notify Fort Smith myself about what's going on at the Open A. And while I'm in town I'll buy some provisions. But while we're waiting, tell me a bit more of what that man told you about Nelson's place.'

'It's a group of buildings standing on the top of a flat-topped hill, with a good clear view in every direction,' said Brad, 'and it's surrounded by a tall barbed-wire fence, with only one gate in it, manned by a couple of guards twenty-four hours a day. As for the buildings, there was a saloon and general store, as well as a blacksmith shop and livery stable, and a lot of accommodation for feeding and sleeping the guests. And Nelson has given the place a name. He calls it Nelson's Mount. The nearest town is Brody, ten miles to the south.'

'That's all mighty interesting,' said Jake. 'It looks

like the first thing we should do when we get there is take a good look at that fence in the dark.'

A little later, watching from cover, they saw the two men leave town and disappear from view. Jake rode in and prepared and handed in the telegraph message. Then he went to the store for provisions, a small bundle of fine wire, and a wire-cutting tool, as well as a used pair of field glasses, before rejoining Brad.

They continued to follow the outlaws, and on the next three nights, after midnight, Jake approached the outlaws' camp, but was unable to confirm that Marian was one of the group lying around the fire.

On the morning after the third night, Jake and his companion continued their pursuit. In the early afternoon, watching from cover on the top of a low ridge which ran across their path, they saw that the riders they were following were heading for a group of buildings on a flat-topped hill, about 150 feet high, with gently sloping sides.

'That must be Nelson's Mount,' said Jake.

He trained the field glasses on the group climbing the slope. Near the top they came to a halt, and two men walked towards them. Jake closely examined the stationary riders, and he was sure that he had identified Marian, on the chestnut. A few minutes later the group rode through the gate in the fence and disappeared from view.

'We'd best stay here for now,' said Jake, 'and

watch out for Craven and his men leaving.'

Three hours later, they saw twelve riders leave.

When Craven and the others rode up to the guards at Nelson's Mount, Craven was recognized by them. They looked curiously at Marian.

'I want to see Nelson,' said Craven. 'We'll be riding on after we've had a meal.'

'I'll take you to see Mr Nelson in the house,' said one of the guards. 'The others can go to the saloon.'

'All right,' said Craven, 'but the woman comes with me.'

Craven and Marian followed the guard into the house, where Nelson was seated at a desk in the corner of the large living room. He was a big man, running to fat, with a swarthy, bearded face. He was dressed in dark Eastern-style clothing. Recognising Craven as he came in, he stood up, wondering who the outlaw's companion might be. Craven told his prisoner to sit down on a chair, then he took Nelson to the far side of the room, out of Marian's hearing.

'Me and my men ain't staying,' he said. 'I'm leaving the woman with you. Randle of the Open A figured you could make use of her.'

He went on to tell Nelson of the circumstances in which Marian had been captured, and said that she had refused to say who she was or what she had been doing near the Open A.

'Maybe I can drag that information out of her,' said Nelson. 'She's a good-looking woman. I'll put her to work in the saloon.'

Craven went to join his men, and Nelson sent for Bella Goodnight, a plump, motherly-looking woman in her forties whom he had put in charge of the group of girls employed in the saloon for the entertainment of his guests.

When Bella Goodnight came into the living room, she looked curiously at Marian.

'I've got a new girl for you here, Bella,' said Nelson. 'Don't know her name or anything else about her. Seems like she don't want to talk. Get her started in the saloon as soon as you can. And make her understand that there's no chance at all of her getting away from here. If she tries to escape, she's liable to get shot.'

Bella took Marian to the saloon, and up the stairs to one of a row of four rooms which stretched along one side of the building. Inside the room, Bella sat on the bed, and motioned to Marian to sit on a chair near by.

'This'll be your room,' she said. 'Now maybe you'd like to tell me who you are, and how you come to be here.'

Marian looked at Bella. All through the long ride from the Open A, during which she had not been molested in any way, she had been wondering what was in store for her. Now it was clear that she was destined to join the group of saloon girls working under Bella. And she had no idea whether Jake knew what had happened to her. Her heart sank.

'Where am I?' she asked.

'This is Nelson's Mount,' Bella replied. 'You've just left Nelson, who owns the whole place. And you've no way of getting away from here if Nelson don't want you to leave. The same applies to me and my girls. The nearest town's ten miles away. And there's a fence round the buildings here. You'd better settle down here and do what Nelson wants. A girl can make plenty of money here. And you ain't got much choice.'

Marian decided that she must try to escape, whatever the risks. She would have to find some way of leaving the saloon unobserved.

'My first name's Marian,' she said. 'That's all you need to know. I don't feel like handing out any more information about myself right now. I'd like a bit of time to get used to the idea of working with your girls in the saloon.'

'All right,' said Bella. 'This is your room. You can stay in here alone till tomorrow morning. Then I'll introduce you to the girls. I'll get Ruby to show you the ropes. She's the most popular girl I have here. Meantime, you can stay in this room. It'll be a while since your last meal?'

Marian nodded.

'I'll bring you something now,' said Bella, 'and

more during the evening.'

She left the room, and reappeared ten minutes later with a tray of food and drink.

'I'll be back later,' she said, as she was leaving.

Though she had little appetite for the meal, Marian forced herself to eat and drink most of what Bella had brought. Then she looked round the room. It was small, with a door through which she had entered, and a window in the opposite wall. She walked over to the window, undid the catch, and pushed up the bottom half. Then she poked her head through the opening.

She could see a railed veranda, empty at the moment, running along the wall outside the rooms. Below the veranda ran a narrow passage between the side of the saloon and the adjacent building. She could see no stairs leading from the passage to the veranda. She climbed out through the window, and crossed to the rail. Looking down, she could see that the veranda was supported by four timber pillars. Then, looking along it, she could see, at the end, a door leading into the saloon.

Marian decided that, sometime after midnight, when things had quietened down and most of the people in Nelson's Mount were in their beds, she would leave her room by the window, climb down a pillar to the passage below, and do her best to get through the fence and escape.

NINE

When Jake and Brad saw the group of twelve riders
leave Nelson's Mount without Marian on the chestnut, Jake decided to carry out a rescue attempt as
soon as possible.

'What I aim to do,' he told Brad, 'is get through
the fence after dark and see if I can locate Marian.
Most likely she'll be somewhere in the saloon. I'm
hoping I can walk in there, and pass myself off as
one of Nelson's guests. Then, if I can find out where
Marian is, I'll try and bring her out later in the
night.'

'That's a big risk you'll be taking,' said Brad.
'D'you want me to go in there with you?'

'No,' Jake replied. 'I'd like you to wait outside the
fence for us, with the horses.'

As soon as it was sufficiently dark they left their
cover and rode round Nelson's Mount so that they
could approach the fence at a point remote from

the gate. They rode up the gentle slope, and at the top they found that the fence was not yet visible in the darkness.

'Stay here with the horses,' said Jake, 'while I go take a look at the fence. I'll come back and see you before I go inside.'

Taking with him the wire cutters and the bundle of wire he had purchased on the way from the Open A, Jake walked cautiously forward, and moments later he saw the fence in front of him. At this point it was a short distance from the nearest buildings on the other side.

Jake dropped the items he was carrying on the ground and closely examined the fence. It was stoutly built, just under seven feet tall, with closely spaced timber posts. The horizontal lengths of barbed wire were so firmly fixed, and so close to one another, that it would be impossible to pass between them. The tops of the posts were connected by stout pieces of timber, around which barbed wire had been liberally wound. Without tools, thought Jake, the fence was not an easy obstacle to overcome. He guessed that it was inspected regularly, particularly during the night, for any signs of forced entry.

Then, somewhere along the fence, he heard the sound of a cough. Quickly, he picked up the wire and cutter and retreated until the fence was only just visible. As he lay spread-eagled on the ground, and looking towards the fence, he saw the outline of a man walking slowly along it. And he could hear the sound of a stick being drawn across the wires to check that none had been cut. He waited for a short while after the man had disappeared from view, then went to Brad and told him what he had found.

'I'm going through the fence now,' he said, 'and I'm hoping that when I come back to this spot Marian will be with me. If we're not back half an hour before dawn, you'd best move off out of sight. No sense in you getting caught.'

Leaving Brad, Jake walked back to the fence, reasonably confident that he would be able to work on it for a while without being disturbed. He cut three wires near the bottom of the fence, which allowed him to pass through without difficulty. Then, using the wire he had brought with him, he carefully fastened together the ends of the three wires, so that they were as taut as the undisturbed ones. He was sure that in the dark the fact that the wires had been tampered with would not be noticed. There was a small clump of brush on the rough ground between the fence and the buildings, and he hid the cutter and wire in this. The time was half past nine in the evening.

Jake made his way, unobserved, to a central area around which the buildings stood. He soon identified the saloon, which was brightly lit, and in which he could hear the sounds of a piano being played. He walked up to it and looked inside through one of the windows. The place was busy, with several card games in progress, men standing drinking at the bar, and men and girls sitting drinking at tables.

Jake moved on to the door and went inside. He walked up to a space at the bar and ordered a beer. So far there was no indication that his presence in the saloon was drawing any particular attention to himself. When his drink had been served, he stood with his back to the bar, and looked around the saloon.

He could see five saloon girls, who were entertaining some male customers, and one older woman, Bella Goodnight, who was sitting in one of the card games. There was no sign of Marian. From where he was standing he could see a flight of stairs leading to an upper floor which only partly covered the floor down below. The stairs gave access to four rooms along the side of the saloon, the doors of which were visible to Jake. He guessed that the stairs also gave access to other rooms on the same floor, on other sides of the building.

As Jake watched, one of the girls climbed the stairs with a male companion, turned right and went into the end room. As Jake continued to watch, he saw Bella Goodnight leave the card game and speak briefly to two of the girls. Then she disappeared behind the bar. She came out five minutes later, carrying a tray of food and drink, which she took upstairs and into the second room from the left. A few minutes later she came out and went through the next door on her right. When she came out of the room shortly after, and came downstairs, Jake noticed that she was now wearing a black mantilla around her shoulders.

The indication was, thought Jake, that the woman had just left her own room, and it seemed possible that Marian was in the room to which the tray had been taken. He decided to stay on in the saloon for a while to see if he could get confirmation that Marian was, in fact, in the room upstairs.

He was just about to turn and order another beer when a movement at the swing doors caught his attention. Two men were coming into the saloon. As he recognized one of them his hand went up to scratch his brow and hide his face as he turned round to face the bar. The two men walked up to a space at the bar next to Jake. As they reached it, he turned away from them and walked slowly out of the saloon. It had been a close call. The man he had recognized was a criminal called McAllister. As a lawman in Kansas, Jake had once arrested him for being drunk on the street and firing off his pistol in a manner which threatened the safety of the public. McAllister had been jailed for a spell, and fined, and left Kansas soon after. Later, Jake had heard that McAllister was suspected of being involved in stagecoach robberies in the Texas Panhandle.

Jake walked to the end of the passage, running

along the side of the saloon, which Marian had looked down on earlier. He could see the veranda outside the four rooms he had been watching from inside the saloon. He decided to work on the assumption that Marian was in the room into which the tray had been taken. He would climb up on the veranda later, when the saloon was quiet, and make a rescue attempt. Until then, he would need to hide in a safe place.

He investigated the building on the other side of the passage in which he was standing, to discover that it was the blacksmith's shop, which was in darkness. Unobserved, he walked to the big double door, found it was not secured and pulled open one side. He walked into the shop, closing the door behind him. This, he thought, would be an ideal place for him to wait. With the aid of matches he looked around, and found just what he required. It was a ladder lying on the floor ag'ainst the wall, just long enough to reach up to the veranda.

He kept a check on the activity in the saloon, and at last saw the lights inside go out. He waited half an hour, then carried the ladder into the passage and carefully placed it against the end of the veranda furthest from the front of the saloon. He climbed up the ladder, over the rail, and on to the veranda. Tiptoeing along it, he saw that there was a light in only one of the four rooms, the one which he thought might be occupied by Marian. Praying that his hunch was right, he tapped on the window pane with his knuckle, not so loudly that the sound could be heard in the adjoining rooms.

Inside the room, Marian, fully dressed, and just about to approach the window to embark on her attempt to escape from Nelson's Mount, heard the tapping on the window and froze. She could think of only one person who would be out there, trying to draw her attention. Praying that she was right, she picked up the lamp, walked to the window, and raised the blind, to see Jake looking in at her from outside. Hastily, she put the lamp down, undid the window catch, and raised the bottom half. As it moved upwards there was a screeching noise. Jake climbed through the open window into the room, and pulled the blind down behind him. He turned to Marian.

'Can't tell you how glad I am to see you,' she said. 'I was due to start work in the saloon tomorrow. When you tapped on the window, I was just getting ready to climb out on to the veranda and down to the ground. Thought maybe I could find some way out through the fence.'

'I took a guess you were in this room,' said Jake, 'and I'm sure glad I was right. We'd best get moving. We'll have no trouble getting through the fence. And on the other side we'll find two horses and a friend of mine.'

They both started to move towards the window,

when suddenly the door of the room opened, and Bella Goodnight, who had been disturbed by the sound of the window sliding up, stood in the opening. She was wearing a dressing-gown over her night-clothes. Jake, who had drawn his six-gun, pointed it in her direction. Bella stepped into the room, and closed the door behind her. She pointed at the revolver in Jake's hand.

'No need for that,' she said. 'It could be that I'm on your side. I can't imagine just how you got into Nelson's Mount, but can I take it you're a friend of Marian here, and you came in to take her away?'

'That's right,' said Jake.

'I don't think it's right,' said Bella, 'for Nelson to force a woman to work here as a saloon girl against her will. Me and my girls all chose to come here, but we didn't know then that he wouldn't let us leave if we wanted to move on. Tell me, if you do manage to escape with Marian, will you let the law know about Nelson's operation here? I expect you know he's hiding criminals?'

'We know,' said Jake, 'and I can promise you that if we get away, Nelson is finished here.'

'That's what I wanted to hear,' said Bella. 'Anything I can do to help?'

'Just go back in your room,' said Jake. 'We'll be all right.'

'Good luck,' said Bella, and returned to her room.

Jake and Marian left through the window and climbed down the ladder, which Jake carried back into the blacksmith's shop. Then he and Marian made their way towards the section of fence through which Jake had passed earlier. On the way, he retrieved the wire cutters and wire, and once again he cut three wires, this time to allow himself and Marian to pass through. He had just finished joining up the ends of the cut wires, when he saw, through the darkness, the figure of a man approaching the other side of the fence. The man, Dalton, was coming from the bunkhouse to start a routine check of the fence. He was carrying a stick and a Winchester rifle.

Spotting the two figures on the other side of the fence, he dropped the stick and raised the rifle. Jake picked up the cutters and wire with one hand and grabbed Marian's arm with the other. Crouching down, they ran away from the fence, with Dalton firing at them. As Jake felt a rifle bullet graze the side of his hip, Marian tripped and fell down. Jake fell with her, twisted round, and sent two carefully aimed bullets from his six-gun into the man on the other side of the fence. He saw Dalton go down. He led Marian towards the place near by, where he had left Brad earlier.

They had only covered ten yards or so when they came upon the body of Brad lying on the ground. Jake knelt down over him, to find that he was dead, shot through the head. He guessed that Brad, hearing the gunfire, had been moving up with the idea of helping them when, by a cruel twist of fate, a stray bullet had ended his life.

'He's dead, Marian,' said Jake. 'Shot through the head. There's nothing we can do for him. We'd best be moving. They'll be coming after us soon.'

They moved on to where the two horses were standing, mounted them and headed south, towards Brody, taking the wire and cutters with them.

The sound of gunfire at the fence raised the alarm, and it was not long before Dalton was discovered, lying on the ground against the fence. Hit in the chest, he had just time to tell the men who found him that he had seen two people on the other side of the fence, who had run off when he approached. He had fired half a dozen shots at them, and one or both of them might have been hit. Before he could pass on any further information he died.

Nelson ordered some men to search the area just outside the fence, and Brad's body was quickly discovered. It was brought into the blacksmith's shop. The body was not recognized by Nelson or any of the hands. It seemed that one of the people seen by Dalton at the fence had been killed by him, and the other one had run off, possibly wounded.

Then, just after daybreak, a hand who had been

on a routine inspection of the fence, ran to report to Nelson in the house that three wires in one section of the fence had been cut twice. Nelson hurried back with him to the fence, and inspected the wires.

'It's clear,' he said, 'that one or more people have passed through the fence in both directions during the night. But who were they and what were they doing here?'

A thought struck him and he hurried to the saloon and knocked on the door of Bella Goodnight's room.

'Where's the new girl?' he asked. 'I want to see her.'

'In her room next door, I reckon,' said Bella. 'I was just going to go in and see her. I'm going to put her to work today.'

Nelson accompanied Bella to the door of Marian's room, and she knocked on it. When the knock was not answered they went inside. The room was empty, and the window was slightly open, with the catch undone.

'Damn!' said Nelson. 'It looks like she's got away. You heard nothing in the night?'

Bella shook her head, and Nelson hurried off. A little later, downstairs, Bella heard from the barkeep that an unidentified man had been shot dead on the other side of the fence, and she went to the blacksmith's shop to take a look at him. Seeing that he was not Jake, she assumed that Jake and Marian had escaped, leaving a dead partner behind.

Realizing the danger if the law came to hear from Marian about the criminal operation he was running, Nelson put all available men on an immediate and widespread search for a woman answering Marian's description, riding alone and possibly wounded. If found, she was to be brought back to Nelson's Mount.

TEN

On the way to the small town of Brody, Jake told Marian about his capture of Brad Lonnigan near the Open A, and of Lonnigan's offer to help him rescue her.

'If it hadn't been for him,' said Jake, 'I wouldn't have known that Craven was bringing you to Nelson's Mount. We owe him a lot.'

They arrived at Brody not long after daybreak, and rode up to the livery stable, where Harper, the liveryman, was opening the big double doors. He looked curiously at the two strangers as they dismounted.

'Howdy,' said Jake. 'We aim to stay in town a short while. Will you feed and water these horses?'

'Sure,' said Harper, 'and if you feel like a meal you can eat pretty good at the hotel along the street there.'

'Thanks,' said Jake. 'We'll do that. But first, we'd

like to have a talk with the most trusted and respected man in town. Who d'you reckon that would be?'

Surprised at the question, Harper looked closely at both of them before he replied. 'I don't need no time to think about that,' he said. 'The answer is Doc Warren. He's doctored pretty well everybody in town over the years, And if he knows a patient is having a run of bad luck and is struggling to make ends meet, he don't charge any fee.'

'Sounds like a good man,' said Jake. 'Where will we find him?'

'Next door to the hotel,' Harper replied.

Leaving the horses, Jake and Marian walked along to the doctor's house and knocked on the door. It was opened by a sprightly, cheerful-looking man in his fifties, bearded, and around average height. He smiled at them.

'Good morning, folks,' he said. 'What can I do for you?' You both look pretty healthy to me.'

'It ain't our health we're bothered about,' said Jake, 'though I've got a bullet graze on my hip that maybe you'll look at later. We've got something more important to talk about, and it's urgent. Can you spare is a little time?'

Intrigued, Warren beckoned them in, and led them to his living room, where they all sat down. Warren listened with keen interest while Jake and Marian told him of their pursuit of Craven, the

111

reasons for it, and Marian's recent experience at Nelson's Mount, which was being used as a hideout for criminals.

'We're sure,' said Jake, 'that as soon as Nelson found out that Marian had escaped, he would send men out searching for her. And it ain't going to be long before one or more of them turns up here. On the way here, Marian and I worked out a plan for dealing with the situation, but it needs help from some of the folks in town. We want Nelson to think that Marian has been found dead, with a gunshot wound, just outside town. If he thinks she's got away, it's likely he'll close down his operation at Nelson's Mount and go into hiding before the law catches up with him. But if he believes Marian died before she could speak to anybody, he'll carry on with what he's doing now. And that'll give me time to get in touch with the US marshal at Fort Smith. I reckon he'll be glad of the chance to pick up Nelson and his men, and the criminals they find at Nelson's Mount.'

Jake went on to describe the plan he and Marian had in mind.

'That's a good plan,' said the doctor, 'and I know the two men who can make it work. I've got to say, I'm looking forward to this. Things have been a bit dull around here lately. Wait here. I'll be back soon.'

He left, and returned ten minutes later with

Kemp, the barkeep at the saloon, and Sawyer, the blacksmith. He introduced them to Jake and Marian. Then he explained the situation to the two townsmen, and said what he wanted them to do. Both men readily agreed to take part, and after a short discussion on the details they returned to their places of work.

'There's a room in the house here,' said the doctor, 'that gives a good view of the street and the saloon doors. We all agreed that anybody riding in from Nelson's Mount, and looking for information, would make a beeline for the saloon. You two can wait in there and watch out for them.'

It was just before noon when Franklin, one of Nelson's hands, rode into town alone and went into the saloon. Marian identified him as one of the guards she had seen on her arrival at Nelson's Mount. Jake told the doctor this, and Warren hurried over to the saloon. He gave the signal to the barkeep that the stranger who had just come in and was facing him over the bar, was from Nelson's Mount. Then the doctor went to see the blacksmith, to tell him of Franklin's arrival at the saloon, before returning to join Marian and Jake at his house.

In the saloon, Franklin was the only customer. He asked Kemp for a beer, then commented on how hot it was outside. He swallowed half the contents of his glass before speaking again.

'I ain't been here before,' he said. 'Right now,

I'm on my way to Texas. This sure is a quiet peaceful kind of a town. The sort of place I'd like to live in when I'm getting old. I guess you don't see many strangers around here?'

'You're right there,' said Kemp. 'Only two strangers I can recall in the last two weeks. One is yourself. The other is the dead woman who was found just outside town early today.'

Franklin stared at him. 'A dead woman!' he said. 'And nobody knew her?'

'That's right,' said the barkeep. 'She was lying dead on the ground, with a bullet in her back. Her horse was standing near by. Nobody in town had ever seen her before. Good-looking woman, she was, and likely in her twenties, with nothing on her to say who she was. It's a real mystery, how she come to be there.'

'She'll be buried in town, then?' said Franklin.

'That's right,' said Kemp. 'This afternoon. The blacksmith's tending to all that. He's our undertaker.'

Franklin quickly finished his drink and left the saloon. He stood by his horse for a short while, thinking up an excuse to go in the blacksmith's shop, where he might get a chance to see the body of the woman found dead that morning. Then, unaware that three pairs of eyes were watching him from the doctor's house, he walked his horse along the street to the smithy, tied it to the hitching rail,

114

and went inside. His eyes were immediately drawn to a medium-sized plain coffin, with lid in place, which was standing on two trestles near one wall of the shop. Sawyer, a big man, with powerful arms and massive shoulders, was standing by his anvil. Franklin walked up to him.

'Howdy,' he said, pulling a knife from a sheath on his belt. 'I've got me a knife here that don't cut like it should. Figured maybe you could sharpen it up for me?'

'Sure,' said the blacksmith. He took the knife over to a grinding wheel, where he worked on it for a short while, then handed it back to its owner. Franklin paid him, then looked over at the coffin.

'Just heard in the saloon about the dead woman being found,' he said. 'I guess that's her coffin over there.'

'That's right,' said Sawyer. 'I just finished nailing the lid down. It's a sad business. A woman dying like that, and no kin or friends here to see her buried.'

'It sure is,' said Franklin. 'I'll be on my way.'

He rode out of town to give Nelson the good news, confident in the belief that Marian posed no threat to the operation at Nelson's Mount. Shortly after Franklin's departure, Kemp and Sawyer walked to the doctor's house to join him and his two visitors. They told them what had happened, and Sawyer said he was sure that the rider from Nelson's Mount had left town in the firm belief that Marian was dead.

'We're real obliged to you all for what you've done,' said Jake.

'We were glad to help,' said the doctor, 'and you can be sure that nobody from Nelson's Mount ever learns of the trick we pulled on them today. Generally, we have no dealings with them. They get all their supplies in by freight wagon from over the border. What are you two aiming to do now?'

'In the morning,' said Jake, 'we head south after Craven and his men. We know they were aiming to cross the Red River into Texas when they left Nelson's Mount, and while they were holding Marian prisoner she happened to overhear two of them talking about a Bar 10 Ranch and a place called Bixby. There's a chance that Craven and the others were heading for that ranch. We'll cross the Red and see if we can find it.'

'I can help you with that,' said the blacksmith. 'I've been to Bixby. It's due south of here, about twelve miles south of the Red River. I have a twin brother there, who runs the livery stable. He would know if there's a ranch called the Bar 10 anywhere in that area. I'll give you a letter asking him to give you any help he can. I'll bring it to the hotel later.'

Jake thanked Sawyer, who left with the barkeep. Then the doctor attended to the flesh wound on Jake's hip before he and Marian went to the hotel.

They rode out of town early the following morning, crossed the Red River in the afternoon, and headed for Bixby. They arrived just before dark, and soon found the livery stable. They stopped outside it, dismounted, and went inside. Matt Sawyer came out of one of the stalls and walked up to them. He was an almost exact replica of his brother in Brody. Jake introduced Marian and himself, and handed the liveryman the letter from his brother, which he read with interest.

'Any help I can give, you're welcome to,' he said. 'I'll bring your horses in, and then we'll go to my house next door. You can take supper with Ella and me, and tell us all about your problem.'

Sawyer attended to the two horses, then took Jake and Marian out through the rear door of the stable, and along to the back door of the house. He led them inside to meet his wife Ella, a small attractive woman, dwarfed by the size of her husband. Sawyer showed her the letter. She read it, then spoke to Jake and Marian.

'I can whip up a meal for us all pretty quick,' she said. 'I reckon I'll do that, and we can talk after supper about just how we can help you.'

After the meal, which Marian helped Ella prepare, they all sat down in the living room, and Jake and Marian explained the situation fully.

'We think,' said Jake, in conclusion, 'that Craven and eleven of his men arrived at a Bar 10 ranch in this area maybe two days ago. D'you know of a Bar 10 ranch around here?'

'We sure do,' Matt replied. 'The ranch house is about seven miles west of here. The owner died a while back. His daughter, who lives back East, inherited the place, and decided to sell it. It ain't been worked for a while, but some men turned up two days ago to get the ranch running again. A couple of them were in town this morning. I don't know if the new owner's name is Craven or not.'

'With the law after him in Texas,' said Jake, 'he could be using another name here. The first thing we've got to do is make absolutely sure that Craven is at the Bar 10. Once we know that for sure, I'm going to take the stage to Fort Worth and ask the Texas Ranger captain there to send a posse to arrest Craven and the others.'

'It's clear,' said Matt, 'that you both need to stay inside our house for the time being. You can't risk being spotted and recognized by somebody from the Bar 10 who knows you. We've got plenty of room. I reckon there's a good chance that somebody from the Bar 10 will ride in tomorrow. If you watch from a room at the front overlooking the street, maybe you'll see Craven or one of his men. That'll prove that it *is* Craven who's taken the Bar 10 over.'

'We'll do that,' said Jake, 'and we're mighty obliged for your help.'

The following morning, Jake and Marian kept watch, from the liveryman's house, on the street outside. They had not long to wait before a Bar 10 hand rode into town. As he came into their view, Marian recognized him immediately as one of the men who had accompanied her from the Open A to Nelson's Mount. She had heard one of the other hands call him by the name Nolan. She told Jake this, and they watched while Nolan went to the store, then the saloon, and eventually rode out of town, an hour before noon, in the direction of the ranch. They gave the news to the liveryman and his wife.

'So what we have to do now,' said Jake, 'is make sure that Craven is at the Bar 10, before we call in the law.'

'I've been thinking about that,' said Matt. 'What I'll do in the morning is ride to the Bar 10 for a talk with the owner, if he's there. I'll tell him that if he's thinking of buying some quarter horses for his cowhands when he gets some cattle on the ranch, I can put him in touch with the owner of a horse ranch east of here where he'd get first-class animals at a reasonable price. And that's something I could actually do, if it came to it. The owner of the horse ranch is a friend of mine, and I've steered a few orders in his direction in the past.'

'We wouldn't want you to put yourself in any danger on our account,' said Jake.

'Can't see how I'd be in any danger,' said Matt. 'When a ranch is starting up, it's natural that folks around will be looking to do business with it. But before I go, I'll need to have a good description of Craven.'

Jake could see that Matt was set on going to the Bar 10. He gave him a detailed description of Craven.

The liveryman rode out the following morning, leaving Ella in charge of the livery stable. He returned around noon, and came into the house to see Jake and Marian.

'Craven's there all right,' he said, 'only now he calls himself Penny. Apart from everything else, I saw that small scar on his temple that you mentioned. He was pretty short with me. Said he didn't want to talk business with anybody right now. I didn't see no cattle around. I spotted a few hands. There were probably more inside the buildings.'

'That settles it, then,' said Jake. 'I'll take the next stage west. It'll be a lot quicker that way.'

'Take the evening stage,' said Matt, 'and you'll be able to talk with somebody at the Texas Ranger's office in Fort Worth tomorrow morning.'

The stagecoach arrived in Fort Worth on time, and after taking a meal Jake walked along to the office of the Texas Rangers, and asked to see the captain. He was shown into a room where Captain Stewart was seated behind a desk. Stewart was a tall lean man in his fifties, with a neat black moustache and a keen eye.

Jake introduced himself and told the captain about the pursuit of Craven and his men by himself and Marian, and the reasons for it.

'I heard about the raid on the Box C,' said Stewart, 'and I knew you'd followed Craven into the Indian Territory.'

'We followed him right through the territory and into Texas,' said Jake. 'He's taken over the Bar 10 ranch near Bixby, east of here. He has maybe eleven men with him. I figured you'd want to send a posse to pick them up.'

'You figured right,' said Stewart. 'We have a big operation under way near San Antonio right now, but it should be over in a couple of days. Then I'll send a posse along to Bixby. They'll arrive after dark, contact you at the liveryman's house, and raid the Bar 10 during the night. As far as you know, Craven and his men will still be there?'

'As far as I know,' said Jake, then went on to tell the captain of the operations at the Open A and Nelson's Mount in the Indian Territory.

'Hold on,' said Stewart, before Jake had finished. 'There's a federal marshal in town. He should be told about this. Let's go see him.'

They left the building, and walked to another office a little way along the street. They found US Marshal Hardy inside. He was about the same age as Stewart, but shorter and broader. He was known as a fearless and tenacious peace officer, with many years of law enforcement behind him. He listened closely as Jake told of the use of the Open A and Nelson's Mount as hideouts for criminals.

'This is mighty interesting,' he said, 'because it gives us a chance to pick up a fair number of badly wanted criminals in two operations. These will have to be organized from Fort Smith. But the matter's so important, I'm going to take the next stage there, so's I can pass the information on, and join the operation myself. So while you're here, I'd like you to tell me everything you can think of about the Open A and Nelson's Mount.'

When Jake had done this he took the next stage back to Bixby, to await the arrival of the posse.

ELEVEN

Jake arrived back in Bixby during the morning of the day after his talks with Stewart and Hardy in Fort Worth. He told Marian and the Sawyers what had happened there.

'So now,' he said, 'all we have to do is lie low, and wait until the rangers get here.'

At midday, the Sawyers, with Marian and Jake, sat down for a meal. When they had finished it, the women cleared up, then prepared to hang out some laundry on a clothes' line just outside the back door of the house. At the same time, Nolan was dismounting outside the stable. He had a message for Matt from Craven, to say that the rancher would like Matt to ride out sometime to discuss the purchase of some quarter horses that he would now be needing sooner than he had expected.

Nolan walked into the stable, but could see no

123

sign of the liveryman. He went to look in the stalls at the back of the stable, but there was no one there. Glancing out of a small window at the side of the stable, he saw two women come out of the back of the liveryman's house, with a basket of laundry. He turned away, with the intention of going to ask them where he could find the liveryman. Then he turned back. There was something familiar about one of the women. He studied her closely through the window, and quickly realized that she was the woman they had taken from the Open A to Nelson's Mount. Even the clothes she was wearing were the same. Shocked, he quickly left the stable, and rode back to the Bar 10. He found Craven in the ranch house, and told him the disturbing news.

'You sure it's her?' asked Craven.

'Plumb sure,' Nolan replied.

'I don't like this,' said Craven. How did she get away from Nelson? What is she doing here? Does she know we're at the Bar 10? Maybe she's already seen and recognized somebody from the ranch in town. The woman could be a danger to all of us. Take four men with you, and go into town after dark. Pick up the woman, and bring her back here. We've got to find out from her what she's doing here, and whether we're in any danger from the law. Wear masks, and tie up and gag anybody else in the house.'

It was mid-evening when Nolan and his four

companions rode into town. They kept off the main street, and approached the liveryman's house from the rear. Inside the house, supper was over, and the Sawyers and their guests were sitting in the living room at the rear of the house. Nolan and the others dismounted, and the rest held back while Nolan crept up to a window where light was showing through a gap in the curtains. Immediately, he saw Marian. She was seated in a chair, facing the window. Then he glanced at a man sitting in another chair by her side. His jaw dropped as he recognized Jake, whom he had last seen when he was being held captive on the Box C. He realized that the situation could be even more dangerous than they had supposed, and he knew that Craven would want both Bannister and the woman to be taken back to the Bar 10. Looking around the room, he could see the liveryman and his wife, also seated. He went back to the others, and told them of the new development.

'Our best way in is through the back door,' he said. 'We'll batter it down and rush them before they can get hold of any weapons.'

They looked around and found a chopping block, long enough for two men to hold it firmly. They put on their masks, then two men took hold of the block and stood a few paces from the wall of the house. Then they ran up and smashed the end of the block against the door, which instantly burst

125

open. With guns drawn, they all ran through an open door into the living-room.

At the sound of the impact the four people in the room sprang up, but a moment later, with five guns trained on them, they realized that resistance was futile. Nolan ordered them to sit down. Then he spoke to Jake.

'You'll be taking a ride with us, Bannister,' he said. 'You and the woman.'

They bound the Sawyers tightly to their chairs, and gagged them. Marian and Jake were then gagged, and their hands were bound. They were taken to the rear door of the stable. Two of Nolan's companions went inside, saddled two horses which, by chance, were the ones belonging to Marian and Jake, and led them outside. The prisoners were ordered to mount, and were led away from the buildings, and out of town, before heading in the direction of the Bar 10. When they reached the ranch, Nolan and another hand took the prisoners into the ranch house to see Craven. At sight of Jake, the outlaw's eyebrows shot up and he stared at the prisoner in shocked surprise. He turned to Nolan, who told him how they had found Jake at the livery-man's house with Marian.

Looking at the two prisoners, with his mind working overtime, Craven reasoned that their presence in Bixby together, so near to the Bar 10, must be more than a coincidence. He felt a strong premonition of danger. He cursed inwardly. On hearing that the Bar 10 was for sale, he had bought it a few weeks previously, in case things ever got too hot for him at the Box C, and it had since proved to be an opportune purchase. But now it seemed that he and his men were in danger once again. He turned to Nolan.

'We're leaving the ranch,' he said. 'And I mean just as soon as we can. Tell the men that, and say that each one has to carry as many provisions as he can. Tell them to be ready to leave in one hour.'

'Where are we going?' asked Nolan, 'and what about these two?'

'Out of Texas,' said Craven, 'and they'll go with us. We'll ride north and cross the Red into the Indian Territory. You remember that big cave we saw on the way down here, not far north of the river? We'll hide out there for the time being. And when you've spoken to the men, send Ford in to see me.'

When Ford came in, Craven told him to find a place east of the Bar 10 from which he could watch to see whether the ranch was raided by the law. If there was evidence of this, he was to ride to the cave to tell Craven. If nothing happened during the next seven days, he was to leave, and join the others at the cave.

The party, including the two prisoners, who had not been addressed by Craven since their arrival at the Bar 10, reached the vicinity of the cave before dawn. Craven sent two men ahead to confirm that it was empty. Then they all went inside and two oil lamps were lit. Jake and Marian, hands still bound, were ordered to sit down with their backs against the wall. They looked around.

The hard floor of the cave was roughly circular, and about twenty-four feet in diameter. The height of the ceiling varied between seven and nine feet. The wall of the cave was continuous, except for the entrance from outside, and a gap in the wall leading to a narrow passage leading away from the interior of the cave.

Craven took a lamp and walked through the gap in the wall and along the passage. He stopped abruptly as he saw a big hole in the floor just in front of him. Beyond the hole, the passage came to a dead end. He looked down into the hole, which appeared to have vertical sides, and could hear the sound of running water. He returned to the cave and stood in front of the two prisoners.

'Well, Bannister,' he said. 'I don't expect you or your friend here would like to tell me just how you two came to be together in Bixby?'

They both remained silent.

'I thought not,' said Craven. 'But maybe we can change that. That sure is a good-looking woman you've joined up with, Bannister. But whether she stays that way is going to be up to you. I've got a man with me who's real mean, and handy with a knife. If you don't give me the information I want, I'll get him to do some work on her face. But that's going to have to wait till tomorrow. I've got other business to tend to first.'

He rode off shortly after, and the two prisoners were kept inside the cave, seated on the floor with their backs to the wall, and with their hands and feet bound.

'I know things don't look good, Marian,' said Jake. 'Once they think they've got the truth out of us, they'll kill us for sure. We've got to try and escape before daylight tomorrow. We've got to grab the slightest chance to get away.'

'Right,' said Marian. 'If the time comes, I'll be ready. When I joined up with you I knew the risks we were taking.'

During the afternoon Nolan brought into the cave a simple lattice of freshly cut pieces of timber, tied together with rope. He stood it up against the gap in the wall of the cave which led to the narrow passage. It covered the gap with an inch or two to spare on either side, and a little more at the top. Nolan took the lattice out and returned with it ten minutes later. He stood it up against the gap again, and Jake and Marian noticed that the top horizontal bar was lower than before. Nolan left the lattice standing in position, and turned, grinning, to the prisoners.

'I guess you're wondering what this is for,' he said. 'Mr Craven told me to fix up a cell to keep you two in at night. You'll both be tied hand and foot, and put in the passage there. And just in case you did get free, I've built that to keep you in the passage.' He pointed to the lattice. 'We'll put a cooking pot up there, straddling the top of that and that narrow ledge on the wall behind it. That means you can't get into the cave without the pot falling on the floor and waking all the men sleeping in here. So it would be a real fool thing for you to do.'

Late in the evening the prisoners were dragged into the passage with their feet bound, and their hands and wrists so firmly tied together that there was no possibility of either of them freeing the other. They were left lying on the floor. Craven had not returned, and the prisoners had gathered, from conversations they had overheard, that he was not expected back till after dawn. They had also learnt that a guard, relieved every four hours, was stationed outside the cave entrance. Inside the cave, which was lit by an oil lamp, the men lay down on their bedrolls, with their six-guns close by.

The passage was dimly lit by light from the cave passing through the lattice, which had been placed in position, with the cooking-pot at the top.

The prisoners sat up, and Jake told Marian to stay where she was, while he investigated the passage. Slowly, he inched his way along it, and saw the hole

130

in the floor, and heard the running water below. He made his way back to Marian and sat beside her.

'There's only a few yards before the passage ends,' he said, 'but there's a hole in the floor big enough to climb down into. And under the hole I can hear the sound of running water. It's just possible, if we can climb down through that hole, that we can get away from here.'

He told Marian what he had in mind, then sat with his back to the wall.

The surface of the wall was hard, and he felt with his fingers for any sharp projection, at the right height, against which he could rub the rope around his hands and wrists. He knew that if he could sever one of the turns, his hands would come free. Slowly, he worked his way along the whole of one side of the passage, without success. He moved to the other side, and halfway along it, almost opposite the point where Marian was sitting, he found what he wanted. It was a projection several inches long, with a vertical edge sharp enough for his purpose.

'I've found what I wanted,' he whispered to Marian. 'I'm starting on the rope now, but it's going to take a while.'

Holding the rope against the sharp edge, he started moving his hands up and down. He had to stop frequently for a rest, and the pain in his arms and shoulders became more and more intense. Also, his hands started bleeding, from contact with

131

the wall. He guessed that he had been working on it for over an hour before, at last, the rope parted. He rested only briefly, then took off the rope around his ankles. He stood up, and freed Marian.

'You remember, Marian' he said, 'that we saw a man going out to guard the cave entrance just about three and a half hours ago, as near as I can guess. That means he's going to be relieved soon. Either he or the man relieving him will likely look at us through the lattice there. We'd better lie down as though we're both still tied up. Then, as soon as the guard who's been relieved settles down, we'll see if we can find some way out of here.'

Half an hour later, lying on the floor of the passage, Jake saw a man who looked briefly in at them, before moving out of sight. Half an hour later, Jake and Marian rose to their feet and moved up to the lattice. Jake had noticed earlier several coils of rope laid on top of one another on the floor of the cave, close to the entrance to the passage. Marian took a firm hold of the top of the lattice to stop it from moving, while Jake put his arm through it and took hold of the end of a coil of rope lying on top of the pile. Slowly and carefully, he pulled it through the lattice, praying that it would not get tangled as it came out of the coil. But it came freely, and eventually he had the whole length of rope inside the passage.

Carrying this with them, Jake and Marian moved

132

along the passage to the hole. Jake had earlier noticed a rocky, pillar-like projection on the floor of the passage, close to the hole. It was about eight inches in diameter and ten inches tall, with fairly smooth sides. He took hold of it and checked it for firmness. He decided it was suitable for his purpose.

'I'm going to lower you down this hole, Marian,' he said. 'Then I'll come down after you. If we can follow that running water, maybe we can find a way out of here. Are you willing to try?'

'Of course,' said Marian. 'Seems we don't have any choice.'

'Right,' said Jake. 'When you reach the bottom, I'll feel the weight go off the rope. You feel around and see if it's possible to follow the water. If it is, give three pulls on the rope and I'll come down after you. If it's hopeless, give six pulls, and I'll get you back up here.'

He tied the rope around Marian's chest, under the armpits, and wound a turn of the rope around the pillar. Using this as a brake, he was able to lower Marian slowly down to the bottom of the hole. He felt the weight go off the rope, then there was a gentle pull on it as Marian moved around down below. It was several minutes before he felt three tugs on the rope. He tied a loop at his end of it, and dropped it over the pillar. Then he climbed down the rope to reach Marian, where she was standing, in pitch darkness, in about six inches of water.

'The water's running down through a tunnel,' she said, 'and where it starts here it's big enough to go through on hands and knees, with our heads above water.'

'Good,' said Jake. 'Let's see where it leads us.'

He untied the rope around Marian, grasped it in one hand, and swung his arm upward in an effort to free the rope from the pillar above. He was successful at the fourth attempt, and the loop fell down through the hole. He coiled the rope, then, carrying it with him, he crawled along the tunnel on his hands and knees, with Marian following behind. They proceeded in this manner for a while, until the tunnel started to narrow, and Jake had just decided that he would have to lie down in the water, in order to proceed any further, when suddenly he realized that there was a clear space above his head.

Slowly, he straightened up to his full height, then moved to allow Marian to stand up beside him. Feeling around, he discovered that they were standing in a wide vertical crack in the rock above them. The crack extended upwards, beyond his reach. He looked up into it, and stiffened as he thought he saw faint glimmers of light above.

'Look up, Marian,' he said. 'Do you see anything up there?'

Marian stared upwards for a short while, before she replied.

'I think I can see little spots of light up there,' she

said, 'but they're very faint.'

'That's how it looked to me,' said Jake, 'and I reckon I know what it is. It's moonlight. You'll remember, there was a moon showing last night. I'm going to try and climb up there. This crack's narrow enough to let me spread my legs and find a foothold on both sides, provided there are any footholds to find.'

He ran his hand over both sides of the crack.

'These sides are pretty rough,' he said. 'I think I can make it. But it may take some time. While I'm climbing, you'd best go back in the tunnel. If I fall, I wouldn't like to land on top of you. When I get to the top, you can start climbing, and I'll help you up with the rope.'

He tied the rope around Marian's chest, and fastened the other end to his belt. Marian retreated into the tunnel and Jake started climbing, searching for new footholds as he gradually moved upwards. Twice his foot slipped and he almost fell, but eventually he reached the top of the crack, pushed his way through a clump of brush which had grown over it, and lay on the sloping ground above.

After a brief rest, he rose and gave three tugs on the rope, the signal for Marian to start climbing. As she rose up the crack, he kept the rope tight. Halfway up, she slipped, and Jake held her weight until she found footholds again. When she reached the top she sat down beside Jake. A half moon was shining.

'I sure am glad to be out of there,' said Marian. 'How far d'you think we are from the entrance to the cave?'

'I think we're on the same side of the hill as the cave entrance,' said Jake, 'and not far from it. You can see we're near the bottom of the slope.'

'I suppose,' said Marian, 'that the best thing for us to do is get as far away from here as we can, before they find out we're missing?'

'I'm not so sure about that,' said Jake. 'With ten men or so searching, and with us on foot, they'd be almost certain to catch up with us. I think I have a better idea.'

TWELVE

Taking the rope with them, Marian and Jake moved quietly down the hillside until they came to a six-foot sheer drop to the flat ground below. Jake dropped to the ground, then helped Marian down. He pointed along the foot of the hill.

'The cave entrance must be along there,' he whispered, 'and not too far away.'

They both stared in that direction. Suddenly, they saw a brief spurt of flame as a cigarette was lit. The smoker, as far as they could guess, was about twenty-five yards away.

'That'll be the guard,' said Jake. 'It's a pity about this moon. It ain't going to be easy to get close to him without being seen.'

'Maybe we're in luck,' said Marian, looking up at the moon and the large area of cloud which was slowly approaching it.

'I reckon we've got about two hours before the

guard's relieved,' said Jake. 'That gives us plenty of time to do what we talked about earlier.'

The cloud was now covering the moon, and they moved up a little closer to the cave entrance. Then Jake left Marian, and circled around the guard, at a safe distance, until he reached the foot of the hill again. The guard was now between him and Marian. He moved up towards the cave entrance as far as he could without the risk of being spotted by the man standing there. Then he stood still, waiting.

Five minutes passed before he heard the sound he had been waiting for. It was Marian's faint rendition of 'My darling Clementine'. He heard the sound of a movement at the cave entrance as the startled guard stepped out and turned to face the direction from which the faint sound was coming. Silently Jake moved up behind him, plucked the man's six-gun from its holster, and pistol-whipped him over the side of his head. Then he eased him down as he slumped, unconscious, to the ground. Jake ran towards Marian, quietly calling out her name as he approached. Carrying the rope, they both went back to the unconscious man on the ground. They bound and gagged him, and left him at one side of the entrance. Marian took the rifle standing against the wall.

The horses, twelve in all, were picketed between them and the point where Marian had been waiting. They ran up to them, and saddled their own mounts. Then they roped the reins of the remaining horses together, and led them away from the cave.

'I've got no idea,' said Jake, 'where the nearest town is. Let's ride east, and hope one turns up before long. I'd sure like to get in touch with the law soon, so's we can catch Craven's men while they're still afoot. I reckon it won't be long before they find out we're missing, and leave the cave to get hold of some horses.'

They had ridden just over ten miles when they spotted the small town of Bonawa in the distance, ahead of them. Then, a moment later, they saw a group of nine riders rapidly approaching them from the south east. They stopped, to await their arrival. As they rode up and came to a stop, Jake and Marian saw that they were all deputy US marshals. The lawmen looked curiously at the couple and the horses they were leading.

'Howdy,' said Jake. 'We're sure glad to meet up with you. These horses belong to a gang led by an outlaw called Craven. Maybe you've heard of him? They're afoot about ten miles west of here.'

Deputy Garner, who was leading the posse, looked hard at Jake and Marian before he replied.

'I'm guessing,' he said, 'that your name's Bannister. And that's Miss Redford with you.'

'That's right,' said Jake.

'We heard all about you from Marshal Hardy,'

said Garner. 'We're on our way to Nelson's Mount, to pick up all the criminals we find there. The marshal's taking another posse to raid the Open A. He said you and the rangers were going to pick up the Craven gang in Texas. What happened?'

Jake gave the deputies a full account of events since he had left Fort Worth.

'I reckon,' said Garner, 'we should pick up Craven's men while we have the chance. Nelson's Mount can wait for a short while. We'll take the horses with us.'

He looked at Jake. 'We'd be obliged if you'd come along,' he said, 'to show us where the cave is. We've got a good tracker with us. If they've left the cave, we'll follow them.'

'My guess is,' said Jake, 'that they left the cave on foot just about daybreak, that's less than an hour ago. Which direction they would take, I've got no idea. But they *could* be heading towards us.'

'You're right,' said Garner, and he told the tracker to go on ahead, making sure he wasn't seen by the men they were looking for, and come back to alert them if he saw anybody approaching him on foot. Then he turned to Marian.

'I'd be obliged, Miss Redford,' he said,' if you'd ride into Bonawa and send a telegraph message for me to Fort Smith. I need to tell them about the change of plan. When we've picked Craven's men up, we'll bring them straight back to Bonawa, to wait for a jail wagon.'

'Sure,' said Marian. 'I can do that for you.'

While Redford was writing the message, Jake handed Marian a hundred-dollar bill which he normally carried hidden in the lining of his vest.

'I'll get back to you as soon as I can,' he said, 'then we can figure out what to do next.'

Redford gave Marian the message. 'When you've handed that in,' he said, 'go to the hotel. The owner's a good man. Take a room there and wait for us to come back.'

Marian headed for the town and the others followed the faint trail to the west. They had covered about six miles when they saw the tracker riding in their direction. When he reached them he said that he had seen a group of about ten men walking along the trail towards him.

'I reckon they'll be in sight of here in about half an hour,' he said.

A short distance behind the posse the trail passed close by the boundary of a grove of trees, and Garner turned in his saddle to look back at it.

'It seems like we're in luck,' he said. 'We'll hide the horses at the back of that grove, and wait for them inside it, near the trail. Then we'll jump them when they draw abreast.'

Back at the cave, the alarm was raised when the relief guard found the bound man outside, and saw that the horses were missing. Soon, it was clear that the two prisoners had escaped, and Harvey, who was in charge during Craven's absence, considered the situation. He assumed it would be some time before the law would be turning up in search of them. But he had heard of a ravine, east of Bonawa, where they could hide out, and he decided that they would leave the cave immediately, and walk to the ravine, bypassing Bonawa on the way. If the opportunity arose, they would pick up some horses on the way.

Hidden inside the grove, close to the trail, Jake and Garner, with the other deputies, awaited the arrival of Harvey and the others. They had not long to wait before they saw them coming. They were walking in a group, at a steady pace. As they drew abreast of him, Garner gave a command, and suddenly the outlaws were confronted by ten armed men, three of them holding shotguns, who had run out of the grove. Only one outlaw was foolish enough to resist, and he was shot dead before his six-gun was fully clear of the holster. The other outlaws raised their hands in the air.

They were bound, and put on their horses. Then Jake spoke to Garner.

'Craven was due to get back to the cave some time today,' he said. 'I'll ride there and watch out for him.'

'All right,' said Garner. 'I'll send two of the deputies with you. Bring Craven back here if you manage to capture him.'

Harvey and the others were taken towards Bonawa. Just outside town they were ordered off their horses and made to sit on the ground. Garner told one of the deputies to ride to a town fifteen miles to the east, where he knew a jail wagon was kept. The deputy was to arrange for the wagon to be driven to Bonawa, accompanied by a guard. Then Garner rode into town.

He went to see Marian at the hotel, where he found her standing in the lobby with the owner. He told them that the outlaws had been captured, and that Jake and two of the deputies had gone to the vicinity of the cave, where they would lie in wait for Craven, in case he turned up there. He also told them that, with luck, the jail wagon would arrive the following day. Then he went to the telegraph office to send a message to Fort Smith advising of the capture of the outlaws.

Ten minutes before Garner came into town Craven rode in from the east, on his way back to the cave. He had been to see kinfolk near the Arkansas border. He dismounted outside the restaurant, and went in for a meal. He sat down at a table by a window which was near to the door, and which looked out on the street. He ordered a meal, and had just started eating it when he saw a deputy US marshal, unknown to him, pass by the window on the boardwalk outside. The sight of the lawman made him feel uneasy, and he decided to leave town as soon as he had finished his meal.

A little later, he was just about to call for his bill when a townsman came into the restaurant in a state of some excitement, to tell the woman owner and the customers of the presence of the posse and the prisoners being held just outside town. He had the full story of the parts played by Jake and Marian in the capture, and went on to say that it was hoped that the leader of the gang would be captured near the cave.

When the man finished, Craven realized the danger he was in. If Marian saw him in town, and raised the alarm, his chances of escape were mil. He decided that he must leave town immediately. He glanced out of the window, and stiffened as he saw Marian crossing the street, and heading directly towards the door of the restaurant. His hand went to the handle of his six-gun as he watched Marian step up on to the boardwalk, and walk up to the door. Craven pulled his gun out of the holster, and held it out of sight under the table. His gaze was fixed on the door. When it remained closed, he looked out of the window again, and saw that Marian, changing her mind, had turned round, and was walking back across the street. She disappeared into the general store.

Craven holstered his gun, paid his bill, and left the restaurant. Refraining from looking across the street, and partly shielding his face with his hand, he led his horse round to the back of the restaurant, mounted it, and rode, unobserved, out of town. As he cleared the buildings he could see, 200 yards away, the captured outlaws sitting on the ground, with the deputies guarding them. Cursing, he turned his horse and headed east. His destination was the ravine for which Harvey and the others had been heading when they were captured.

As he rode along he reflected with deep anger on the complete collapse of a criminal operation which had been going so well. And all due to the intervention of Jake and Marian. He decided that his first task must be to eliminate the couple once and for all. Then he would start afresh, and build up another criminal organization similar to the one he had led with such success before.

When he rode into the small ravine, which was well away from the few trails in the area, he halted as he saw outside the dilapidated shack ahead of him, a picketed horse. He hailed the shack, dismounted, and approached it slowly with arms upraised. The door opened and a man stepped out, holding a double-barrelled shotgun pointing in Craven's direction. The outlaw recognized him immediately as a man called Snell, whom he had met some time ago during a brief visit to the Open A.

Snell was a man of average height, thickset and bearded, with a ruddy, pleasant face. Despite his normally jovial appearance, Craven knew that he was a vicious and ruthless killer, who was available for hire to anyone with the right kind of money who wanted somebody dead. He also knew that Snell's murderous activities had been so cunningly contrived that he had so far escaped the attention of the law.

With some surprise, Snell recognized Craven, and lowered the shotgun.

'What in hell are you doing here on your own, Craven?' he asked.

'It's a long story,' said Craven. 'Before I tell you, what about yourself?'

'Just finished a job near the Arkansas border,' said Snell. 'I'm heading for Fort Worth, to rest up for a spell. I figured to stay here for the night.'

'It's a stroke of luck meeting up with you like this,' said Craven. 'There's a couple of people near here I want dead. I'm hoping you'll tend to that for me.'

He went on to tell Snell about the intervention of Jake and Marian in his affairs, and the capture of his men.

'I can see why you're pretty riled,' said Snell. 'I'll take the job on. But it's going to cost you.'

'Whatever it takes,' said Craven. 'The woman is

probably in Bonawa right now. And I think it's likely that when I don't turn up at the cave today, Bannister will go back to town with the deputies. He'll probably be there tomorrow. I can't go to Bonawa myself to check on this, in case they see me.'

'I'll ride in tomorrow, then,' said Snell, 'and see if they're both there, and whether they're figuring to stay on for a while. You know how I work. I always do the job away from towns and settlements, and with no witnesses around. That's why I've never been caught. And that's how I want it to stay. I'll work out a plan later.'

THIRTEEN

Jake rode into Bonawa with the two deputies around noon on the day after Craven's men had been captured. They had seen no sign of Craven himself, and thought it was pointless for them to stay there any longer. Soon after they arrived, the jail wagon turned up and the prisoners were put on board, wearing handcuffs and leg-irons. The wagon left a little later for Fort Smith, escorted by an armed guard.

Garner came to see Jake and Marian at the hotel.

'We'll be leaving shortly for Nelson's Mount,' he said. 'I'm sorry we didn't manage to catch Craven. I guess you two are aiming to carry on looking for him.'

'That's right,' said Jake, 'but it's hard to know where to start.'

Soon after Garner and his men had left, Snell rode into town from the east, and went straight to the hotel to book a room for the night. He chatted in the lobby with Ramsey, the hotel owner, for a while. He told him that he was running a freighting business in Fort Smith, and was looking round to see what business he might do in the Indian Territory. Then, from Ramsey, a man who really enjoyed talking with strangers, he got a full account of the recent capture of the outlaws, and the part played in it by Jake and Marian.

'They're staying here,' he said. 'Likely you'll meet up with them.'

'I'd like to,' said Snell. 'I figure on staying here a day or two.'

He took his horse to the livery stable, returned to the hotel, and sat in his room, looking through the window at the street below. It was not long before he heard the sound of people moving in the passage outside his door, and a moment later he saw a man and a woman leave the hotel and go into the restaurant just along the street. He was sure, from descriptions given him by Craven, that they were Jake and Marian.

He waited for five minutes, then left the hotel and followed the couple into the restaurant. He stopped just inside the door, and looked round. Then he walked up to the table where Jake and Marian were seated. He beamed down on them.

'I figure you're Miss Redford and Mr Bannister,' he said. 'I just rode into town an hour ago. I heard all about you from the hotel owner. He said you were set on catching up with an outlaw called Craven who managed to get away. I got to thinking about this, and I remembered something that happened earlier today that might help you. D'you mind if I sit with you, and tell you about it? I'm just about ready for a meal myself.'

'Sure,' said Jake, gesturing towards one of the two empty chairs at the table.

Snell gave them his name, and said that earlier that day he had been riding towards Bonawa from the east. He had strayed well off the trail, and was riding along a small gully when, unexpectedly, he had encountered a man riding in the other direction. They had only exchanged a few words before parting.

'I didn't like the look of him,' said Snell. 'He was a mean-looking man, pretty tensed up, and wearing a six-gun. I didn't like the way he was looking at me, and I was glad when he moved on. I was curious about him, and after a while I sneaked back up the gully and watched him from cover. I saw him ride into a ravine about a quarter of a mile away, and he didn't come out during the next fifteen minutes. So I rode on towards Bonawa. Maybe it's a long shot, but it struck me the man could be Craven. I can give you a description if you like.'

'I'd be obliged,' said Jake. 'Up to now we've had no idea of where Craven might have gone.'

Snell described, in some detail, the man he said he had seen, even down to the small scar on his temple.

'That's Craven,' said Jake, when Snell had finished. 'There's no doubt about it. We'll ride there and see if he's still around. Can you tell us exactly where this ravine is?'

'No,' replied Snell, 'but I could find it in daylight. I'm heading back for Fort Smith tomorrow. I'll show you where it is if you'd like to come along.'

'We'll do that,' said Jake, and went on to ask Snell what he was doing in the area.

'I have a freighting business in Fort Smith,' said Snell. 'I'm looking into the possibility of expanding my operation into the Indian Territory.'

'I reckon it would do well around this area,' said Jake. 'I have a friend in Kansas who runs a big freight company operating through the whole of the state. And he's thinking along the same lines as you. His name's McCarthy. I expect you've heard of him?'

'Of course,' said Snell, and went on to arrange to leave with Jake and Marian early the following morning.

Back in the hotel later, Jake sat with Marian for a while, in her room.

'Maybe we'll be lucky tomorrow,' she said. 'Maybe we can bring this thing to and end.'

'I'm not so sure,' said Jake. 'I have a strong feeling that Snell ain't all he makes out to be. Did you notice how accurately he described Craven. He even mentioned that small scar on the temple, which is only seen properly when Craven isn't wearing a hat. And according to Snell, he was only close to Craven for a minute or two. And that's not all. You heard him say he knew of the McCarthy Freight Company in Kansas. Well, I'm sure there ain't any such company operating there.'

'You think Snell might have been hired by Craven to kill us, or maybe lead us into an ambush?' asked Marian. 'Snell didn't look like a killer to me.'

'You never can tell,' said Jake. 'I'm pretty sure that Craven's involved in this. I reckon we should leave with Snell in the morning. But we need to watch him pretty close, and never let him get behind us. And we've got to watch out for an ambush as well. Is that all right with you, Marian?'

'Yes,' she replied. 'I can see this might be our only chance for a long time of getting close to Craven.'

They left in the morning, an hour after daybreak. Smell was not wearing a sidearm but he carried a Remington 10-gauge shotgun, with double barrels, in a saddle holster. He explained to his companions that he wasn't much good with a sidearm, and he preferred the shotgun because you didn't need to aim it all that well.

Well before noon they reached the gully

mentioned by Snell the previous evening, and stopped halfway along it.

'I'll walk on to the end,' said Snell, 'and see if there's anybody moving near that ravine I saw the man ride into.'

When he came back fifteen minutes later, to report that there was no sign of anyone in the area ahead, they all rode out of the gully and approached the ravine, with Snell slightly in the lead. At Jake's suggestion, they headed for the top of the wall at one side of the ravine, so that they could look down into it, unobserved from below.

A little later, when they were doing this, all they could see was an old shack, with no horses around, or any other sign that it might be occupied.

'It looks like he's moved on,' said Snell. 'But maybe he's left something in the shack that might help you.'

'Let's go and see,' said Jake.

Kneeling in a patch of brush at the top of the slope on the opposite side of the ravine, Craven, who had been waiting there for some time, saw the three riders dismount and look down into the ravine. He watched as they rode along towards the entrance to the ravine. They disappeared from view, and reappeared soon after, riding up the ravine towards the shack. Craven watched them intently, looking forward to the spectacle of Snell blasting into oblivion the two people who had caused his downfall. When discussing Snell's plan with him he had insisted on being able to view the actual killing.

The three riders dismounted near the shack. Jake and Marian stood side by side while Snell walked round his horse and pulled the shotgun from the saddle holster. As he did so, he cocked both the hammers. Then he walked back round his horse to face Jake and Marian. The shotgun was pointing directly at them. His face was bleak.

'Let's have your arms up,' he said, and they both complied.

'I've got to say,' he went on, 'that this is one of the easiest jobs I ever got hired for. You two are finished. The buckshot loads in this shotgun will see to that.'

'Craven hired you, of course,' said Jake.

'That's right,' said Snell. 'And he wanted me to tell you that before you cashed in. Now that's done, let's not waste any more time.'

Jake and Marian were standing close together, and the shotgun was aimed at a point between them which was at a height corresponding roughly with the centres of their bodies. Snell pulled on one of the triggers. He heard the sound of the hammer falling, but there was no explosion. Hastily, he pulled the other trigger, with the same result. Frantically, he dropped the shotgun and reached inside his jacket for the pistol resting in a shoulder holster. He pulled the weapon out, but before he could line it up on either of the couple standing in front of him, Jake shot him in the chest. Snell dropped his pistol, fell to the ground, and lay flat on his back. Jake knelt beside him. From the position of the bullet hole he guessed that the wound was fatal. Snell opened his eyes and looked up at Jake. Then he spoke to him. His voice was barely audible.

'You took the shotgun cartridges out when I left you for a while in the gully?' he asked.

Jake nodded his head.

'Damn you,' said Snell, and a moment later his eyes closed and his head slumped sideways. Jake checked that he was dead.

'We don't know whether Craven's still somewhere around here or not,' he said. 'Let's take Snell's body back to Bonawa. I heard there's a first-class half-breed tracker there who used to work in the army. Maybe he'll come out here and look at the sign, and help us get on to Craven's trail again.'

Looking down into the ravine from his hiding-place, Craven, watching for Jake and Marian to fall, exploded with rage when, instead of this, he saw Snell collapse on the ground and lie still. For a moment he considered firing on the man and woman down below with his rifle, then decided against it. It was too risky. He would kill them himself, but would choose a better time and place very soon. Still seething with rage, he watched as

Snell was lifted on to his horse, which was led out of the ravine by Jake, with Marian riding by his side. Craven assumed they were heading for Bonawa, and a little later, watching them from a distance, he confirmed that they were heading in that direction.

When Jake and Marian reached Bonawa, they handed the body over to the town undertaker. Then, after leaving the horses at the livery stable, they went to the hotel, and told Ramsey what had happened.

'We'll stay here tonight,' said Jake, 'but tomorrow we'll try to get on Craven's trail. I figured that maybe that half-breed tracker I was told about might lend us a hand.'

They went up to their rooms, which could not be locked from the outside, but which had bolts on the inside of the door. Jake went out a little later, to talk with the tracker, who agreed to ride out with them to the ravine the following day. Later, they had supper in the restaurant, before returning to the hotel for the night.

A quarter of an hour past midnight, Craven rode into Bonawa and tied his horse to a post behind the hotel. Inside, he found Ramsey, just about to go to his bed. He told the hotel owner that he was on his way to San Antonio, and only wanted a room for the night. As he signed the register, giving the name of Frost, he saw the names, immediately above his, of

Jake and Marian. Their room numbers were also shown.

In the morning, at daybreak, Craven rose and dressed. Then he sat on a chair by the window, which looked out on to the street. An hour later, he saw Jake and Marian, each armed with a six-gun, leave the hotel and go into the restaurant. Half an hour later they came out, and walked back towards the hotel. Craven left his room and went into the one occupied by Jake. He stood in a position where he would be behind the door when it was opened.

Just outside the hotel entrance, Jake left Marian to make a brief visit to the nearby store. Marian went into the lobby, where Ramsey was standing near the desk. She stopped for a few words with him, and just after he had said that he hoped she hadn't been disturbed by a guest who turned up well after midnight, Jake came in, waved to them, and went upstairs.

'He was a strong-built man, with a real mean look about him,' said Ramsey. 'I. . . .'

He broke off and watched, surprised, as Marian suddenly left him and ran up the stairs, with her six-gun in her hand. She tiptoed quickly along the passage, opened the door of Jake's room, and stepped inside. On the floor, near the bed, Jake was lying on his back, and Craven was kneeling by him with a knife in his upraised hand. He twisted as the door opened, and saw the gun in Marian's hand. He changed his hold on the knife. and drew his arm back to throw it at Marian. But before he had released the knife, the bullet from Marian's six-gun struck his head. He died instantly, and fell across the man he had been about to stab.

Jake, who had received a glancing blow on the head from Craven's pistol, which had temporarily stunned him, came round as Craven fell on top of him. With Marian's help, he pushed the body away and rose to his feet.

'Are you all right, Jake?' she asked.

'A sore head is all,' said Jake. 'I guess you came in just in time. Craven was waiting behind the door for me when I came in.'

Ramsey came up at the sound of the shot, and Jake explained what had happened. The undertaker was called, and the body was removed. The following morning, over breakfast in the restaurant, Marian and Jake discussed the future.

'So it's all over now, Marian,' said Jake. 'We've done what we set out to do. The thing is, we've been close together for quite a while, and if you're of the same mind, I'd like to make it permanent.'

'Is this a proposal of marriage?' asked Marian, smiling. 'No getting down on one knee? No passionate declaration of love?'

'Sorry,' said Jake. 'I guess I could have put it to you better. But I think you know how I feel about you.'

'Exactly the same as I feel about you,' she said. 'But we have a problem. I own a ranch, and so do you. So it seems to me that one of us will have to move in with the other. But which is it to be? Myself, I don't mind one way or the other.'

'In that case,' said Jake. 'Let's make it the Diamond B in Colorado. I know you'll like it there.'

Later in the morning, Jake sent a telegraph message to Fort Smith, advising them of Craven's death, and the death of another man called Snell, according to papers in his pocket, who had been hired by Craven to kill Marian and himself. He also sent messages to the Diamond B and Crazy R, advising that he and Marian were on their way back.

They travelled to the Crazy R by stagecoach, and the wedding took place there. A few days after their arrival, they had a message from US Marshal Hardy, in Fort Worth. It was to say that successful raids had been carried out in the Indian Territory on the Open A and Nelson's Mount, with many prisoners being taken.

Marian gave a share in the Crazy R to her foreman, in return for him running the ranch. And a week after the wedding, she and Jake headed for the Diamond B.